Tiger Boots

Joe O'Brien

THE O'BRIEN PRESS
DUBLIN

First published 2010 by The O'Brien Press Ltd,
12 Terenure Road East, Rathgar, Dublin 6, Ireland.
Tel: +353 1 4923333; Fax: +353 1 4922777
E-mail: books@obrien.ie
Website: www.obrien.ie
Reprinted 2015.
This edition first published 2018 by The O'Brien Press Ltd.
The O'Brien Press is a member of Publishing Ireland.
Reprinted 2018.

ISBN: 978-1-78849-012-2

2 4 6 8 7 5 3
18 20 22 21 19

Layout and design: The O'Brien Press Ltd
Printed and bound in Ireland by Essentra, Glasnevin.
The paper in this book is produced using pulp from managed forests.

www.joeobrienauthor.com

Published in

DUBLIN

UNESCO
City of Literature

Tiger Boots received financial assistance from The Arts Council

Dedication

For all my readers, with humble thanks!

Author's Note

I can't believe we're at book three in the Danny Wilde series. In Danny's words, it's been 'savage' to write another book about all the gang from Littlestown.

A big thanks to all the readers who have sent me kind letters of support and enthusiasm. Please keep them coming!

Once again, I've written lots of fast football action along with plenty of humour and good fun with Danny and his pals, but there are some serious storylines too.

I hope you enjoy reading *Tiger Boots* as much as I've enjoyed writing it.

Joe O'Brien

Acknowledgements

A huge thanks to everyone at The O'Brien Press for all their support and hard work, especially to Helen Carr, my editor; Emma Byrne, for the wonderful book design; Ruth Heneghan for all her hard work promoting the books; Ivan O'Brien, Brenda Boyne and all the sales team for their support and hard work. Special thanks to Mary Webb (Editorial Director) for her continued encouragement and support and, of course, to Michael O'Brien, Publisher.

Sincere thanks to all the supportive booksellers and librarians, enthusiastic teachers and all who dedicate so much of their time to the world of books.

Finally, my biggest thanks go to my wife, Mandy, and my son, Jamie, for their unconditional support, encouragement and love.

Contents

Chapter One

Crokes v Darnville

'**G**o on, Danny!' yelled Jimmy, as Danny Wilde, captain of Littlestown Crokes GAA team, went on a solo.

It was the second half of the home game against Darnville and Danny was playing a cracker of a game. Jimmy, the Crokes assistant coach, was cheering them from the sidelines of their home ground, the Little Croker.

The Crokes were leading by a single point; Darnville had started the second half with a fast pace and had just scored three brilliant points. The Crokes had yet to score in the second half, but Danny was about to change all that.

Jonathon, Danny's cousin and fellow midfielder, called for a pass as he had lost his marker. Danny looked up and swerved a magnificent pass across the middle of the

Little Croker, straight into Jonathon's hands.

The Crokes' number eight then fisted the ball to Paul Kiely, Crokes' right half forward, who lobbed a high ball deep into the Darnville defence.

The ball bounced in front of Crokes' full forward, Doyler, who managed to palm it away from his marker and into the path of Todd Bailey, his centre half forward.

'Todd!' yelled Danny as he ran into a space to Todd's left.

With lightning instinct, Todd fisted the ball over the now exhausted Darnville midfielder who had followed Danny upfield.

Danny caught Todd's pass and, as his marker and the Darnville centre halfback closed in on him, Danny shimmied spectacularly around both players, leaving them eating turf.

Danny then fisted the ball over the Darnville full back and sprinted around him, but the Darnville goal keeper lunged out and just as it looked like he would punch the ball away from goal to safety, Danny Wilde twisted his body around as he leapt into the air and fisted the ball over the Darnville keeper, sending it crashing into the net.

GOAL!

Splinter, Danny's best friend and Crokes' left full forward, jumped on Danny's back.

'Ya mad thing, ya, Danny!'

Mick Wilde (Danny's dad and the team's coach) and Jimmy were jumping up and down on the line.

Mick was always happy when his son scored, but it was even more important to him that his whole team played well, and at the moment, the Crokes were playing fantastic football. They were on a winning streak in the second half of the season and Mick knew that if they could keep it up, they would have a good chance of finishing close to the top of the league table.

The Darnville keeper fluffed his kick out and Todd Bailey pulled off a supreme pick up then sent the ball over the bar. There was no stopping the Crokes now. Darnville's heads dropped and that added fuel to the fire that powered Danny Wilde's team's engine into super-drive.

Crokes hardly let their opponents out of their own half for the rest of the game, which allowed the Littlestown team to score another two points before the referee blew his full-time whistle.

It was a far cry from the early game in the season when Darnville had beaten the Crokes on their grounds, across town in Darnville.

This game ended with a score of 1-9 to 0-5. Two more points in the bag for Mick's team!

Chapter Two

Practice Makes Perfect

Mick Wilde always took mental notes from every game. He didn't need a notebook and pen – everything was stored in his football brain.

For Mick, there was one very positive thing that stuck out in the game against Darnville – the way the build up to Danny's wonderful goal had comprised excellent hand passing between his players.

When Mick gathered his players together at the next Thursday's training, he made sure that they all knew the importance of hand passing in the game of GAA.

Jimmy had just completed a few laps around the outer railing of the park. The roads along the park were well lit and the council had constructed a new foot path all the way around the inner boundary of the park. It created an excellent running track for Jimmy to keep his players super fit.

'Sit down boys and have a breather.' Mick smiled as he looked over toward Jimmy, who had already collapsed on the grass.

'Are we going to have a game of ball, Mick?' asked Paddy Timmons, Crokes' right corner full back.

'In a minute, Paddy.'

Mick gave everyone a few minutes to compose themselves. It was a long way around the park – in fact, it was much longer than Jimmy had imagined when they set out.

Mick took a football to hand, then took one look at his players, and fisted the ball right into the middle of the front row.

Jonathon caught the ball.

'Good catch, Jonathon,' Mick said. 'Hand passing,' he went on, 'I can't emphasise enough the significance of the skill of hand passing, and it *is* a skill. If you can perfect this skill, boys, then you will always have an edge on your opponent. It was a run of brilliant hand passes that led to Danny's goal against Darnville, and the goal itself was fisted in with the hand.'

All Danny's teammates grinned over at him. They appreciated how lucky they were to have such a talented player on the team.

'Everyone on their feet,' instructed Mick.

Poor Jimmy was last up. He had a cramp in his right leg, so Mick told him to walk it off.

'We're going to have a small match now, lads,' said Mick. 'And I want yiz all practising your hand passes.'

Mick set up a small pitch with some cones and gave the boys twenty minutes of football. He made up a few special rules for the game. Everyone had to hand pass every second pass they made with the ball.

Practice makes perfect and Mick was a master when it came to perfecting the game of Gaelic football.

Chapter Three

Danny's Dream

The next morning, Danny and Splinter were having a kick about at break in the schoolyard when Todd Bailey and Billy Stapleton walked over to them.

'Pass, Danny, pass!' shouted Todd, with both hands ready to catch the ball.

Danny still had the previous night's training in his mind and remembered the talk his father had given the team about the importance of hand passing. Danny fisted the ball to Todd who caught it with ease.

'Nice one, mate,' said Todd. 'Here, Billy, catch!'

Todd palmed the ball to Billy, forgetting that Billy Stapleton was no better at football than his horse, Vinny.

Billy caught the ball all right – right in the snot!

Splinter let out a howl.

'You're after bursting his nose!'

Poor Billy's legs almost went from under him as he took his hands away from his face and noticed they were covered in blood.

Just then, Principal Dunstan crept up behind the boys. He arrived so suddenly that it was as if he had appeared out of thin air.

'What's going on here, boys?'

Todd turned to the principal.

'I didn't mean it, sir. It was an accident.'

Danny backed him up.

'Yeah, sir, we were only playing.'

'Yeah!' Splinter added.

Principal Dunstan put his hand on Billy's forehead.

'Pinch your nose, Billy. It's not that bad. Get yourself off to the toilets and wash yourself. It won't look as bad then.'

Then he turned to the others.

'You boys better go with him. He's a bit pale.'

Billy did just as the principal had advised and

when he looked up at the mirror after rinsing his face, he was horrified with what he saw.

Danny, Splinter and Todd burst out laughing.

'It's not funny!' protested Billy. 'My nose is huge!'

It reminded Billy of the very first and last time he'd stepped into a boxing ring; his uncle had encouraged him to take up boxing, and his first practice session had been against Hammer Hughes who was two years older, ten inches taller and thirty-one pounds heavier than him. Hammer had landed a five finger sandwich on Billy's nose and it had ballooned up just the same way.

When Billy told this story to the lads, it only made them laugh even louder.

Danny was in stitches.

'Ah well, Billy. At least you won't have to put a mask on for Halloween next week.'

'Yeah!' added Todd. 'Ya look like an ogre.'

'Yeah. A bit of green paint and a shaved head

and you could be Shrek,' said Splinter.

'Get lost; ya muppet,' Billy said. He was beginning to see the humour in it all. 'I don't have mad looking ears.'

All of a sudden, the laughing stopped and the subject changed in an instant; Splinter suddenly felt the urge to share a dream he had the night before.

'I had a strange dream last night that my ears kept growing and growing.'

Danny, Billy and Todd just stared at Splinter.

'Have you been eating the blue smarties again, Splinter?' Danny joked.

'I'm telling you, lads, it was mental. I thought my ears were going to explode. I could hear noises getting louder and louder.'

'Then what?' asked Todd.

Splinter went a bit red.

'I woke up and my ma was standing over me screaming her head off. I'd had fallen asleep while watching my telly with my ear phones plugged in and turned over halfway through the night, and I accidentally pulled the ear phones out of the socket and the telly woke the whole house up.'

'Ya space cadet, Splinter,' Todd joked.

'It's not funny,' said Splinter. 'My ma nearly had a heart attack and I thought she was going to kill me.'

Splinter's story got the others talking about dreams too – strange dreams.

Billy told them about the time he dreamt that he and his horse, Vinny, were winning the Grand National and with just one jump to go, it all went weird.

'I tucked in tight to Vinny's neck to get him to jump real high,' said Billy, explaining that the last jump was the biggest jump, psychologically. (He actually said 'physicologically', but the lads knew what he was trying to say.)

'What happened next?' asked Danny. They were all intrigued. Billy was a complex character, so they knew that there was going to be something really out of the ordinary coming up next.

And they were right. Billy looked up towards the window as if to let his mind drift beyond the school toilets.

'We jumped and I remember thinking to myself that we were an awful long time in the air. You see lads, I always close my eyes when Vinny does a jump. It's a habit.'

'Are you telling me you've had this dream before?' asked Splinter.

Billy turned around and wiped a little trickle of blood from his upper lip.

'Nearly every night,' said Billy. He smiled, and went on, 'It's all I ever dream of.'

Danny knew were Billy was coming from because all he ever seemed to dream about was playing for the Dubs and lifting the Sam Maguire over his head.

'Go on, Billy,' encouraged Todd. 'What happened next, mate?'

Billy continued.

'Normally it's a deadly jump and we go on and win the National.'

'Did yiz fall, Billy?' asked Danny.

'I wish,' said Billy. This answer confused them.

'What d'ya mean?' asked Todd.

Billy began to explain.

'When I opened me eyes, we weren't even in the race.'

'Where were yiz?' asked Splinter.

'We were in Disneyland and Vinny was one of the horses in the carousel and he kept chewing a boy's coat that was sitting on an elephant in front of us and I thought I was going to puke because I hate carousels and then–'

'Enough!' yelled Splinter. 'You're doing my head in. You're stone mad, Billy.'

'What about you, Todd?' asked Danny. 'Do you ever have any strange dreams?'

Todd quickly delivered an assertive, 'Nah, Mate! We Aussies are totally boring compared to Irish people.'

'What about you Danny?' asked Billy.

Before Danny had a chance to speak,

Splinter answered on his behalf.

'Danny only ever dreams about one thing, and that's playing for the Dubs. Isn't that right, Danny?' Splinter asked.

Danny smiled and nodded.

'Usually,' said Danny. 'But I had a dream the other night and it had nothing to do with football. Well, very little to do with it, anyway.'

'Was it weird, Danny?' asked Billy.

Danny shook his head and laughed.

'I'm not mad like you and Splinter. It was just different. I was on a big aeroplane with my da.'

'Where were you going Danny?' asked Splinter.

'I'm not sure,' Danny answered, trying hard to remember more.

'I just remember dead clearly that I had packed my signed Dubs' jersey, and that was weird. I suppose because that never leaves the wall in my room.'

Todd had a thought on this.

'If it never leaves your room Danny, then

maybe it wasn't a holiday. Maybe you were leaving Ireland for good.'

'Yeah,' agreed Billy. 'Todd's right.'

Splinter changed the subject.

'A few more hours, lads and we've a whole week off. Any special plans?'

Before anyone had a chance to answer, the school bell rang and Principal Dunstan's head peeped inside the door.

'Come on, lads. Back to class. How's the face, Billy?'

'Fine, sir,' answered Billy, and he scurried out of the toilets after the others.

Chapter Four

News from America

On the way home from school, Splinter reiterated his question about the school holidays.

'A whole week off, lads,' he said. 'What are we going to get up to?'

'Not much, I reckon,' answered Todd.

Splinter looked to Danny for a better answer.

Danny just shrugged his shoulders.

'I'm going to a Halloween party in Uncle Larry's next Saturday.'

'No way!' said Splinter. 'Can I come too?'

'I suppose Larry wouldn't mind. I'll clear it with Jonathon at training on Tuesday night.'

'Nice one, Danny. We had a savage time the last time we were there.'

'You'll have to dress up,' warned Danny. 'It's a fancy dress party.'

'No problem, Danny,' said Splinter, and then he turned to Todd, who had been very quiet.

'Are you coming, Todd?' asked Splinter.

Todd was busy texting on his mobile phone.

'Todd!'

'Sorry, mate! Wasn't listening. I was just texting my old mate from my footy club back home.'

'What's his name?' asked Splinter.

Todd pressed the send button and slipped his phone back into his pocket. 'Wayne.'

'Are you coming to Larry's Halloween party next Saturday?' Splinter asked for the second time.

'I don't think so, mate,' Todd said.

'Go on, Todd,' urged Splinter. 'Danny! Can Todd come too?'

'The more the merrier,' answered Danny. 'You might as well, Todd. It'll be savage.'

'Go on then,' Todd said, as they turned onto Danny and Splinter's road. 'But I'm not wearing a stupid costume.'

'We're going into town tomorrow. Do you

want to come along?' Danny asked Todd.

'Nah! I've got to go somewhere with my mum,' answered Todd. 'I'll see yiz at training on Tuesday.'

Todd gave Danny and Splinter a thumbs up, then he headed off home, leaving his two pals in heavy debate as to what costume they would wear to Larry's party.

Danny had Mick's dinner ready for him when Mick arrived home from work. Danny was no cook, but he had been to the chipper and had Mick's favourite in the microwave – a large smoked cod, and chips with curry sauce on the side.

Mick was thrilled. He had been attending a meeting after work and was starving when he arrived home.

'You're a diamond, Danny son,' Mick told him as he tucked into his dinner.

'No worries, Da. I raided the emergency fund. Is that okay?'

'Sure that's what it's there for, Danny,'

answered Mick.

Danny could see that Mick looked weary.

'Is everything alright, Da?'

Mick had to chew quickly on a mouthful of batter before he could answer Danny's question. Then he kind of shrugged.

That said a lot to Danny. Something was wrong.

'What's up?' Danny asked.

'Ah, it's just work, Danny,' answered Mick. 'There's a lot of bad vibes at the moment. You know how it is with this recession.'

'Yeah,' Danny agreed, but he knew his father well and was certain that he was keeping something from him.

He persisted a little more.

'Are you sure that's all?' Danny asked softly.

A tear crept out from Mick's left eye and fell down his cheek, before he could rub it away without Danny noticing.

'I'm okay, son,' said Mick, but his voice trembled.

Danny was really worried now; he moved to the chair beside Mick's and put his arm around him.

Mick turned and smiled, but it was a brave smile – a father's smile. The type of smile that tried its best to protect and say, *'It's all right son. I'm the dad and no matter what, you mean everything to me. You're my life and I'm going to look after you.'*

'It's okay, Da,' Danny soothed.

Mick took a huge gulp of air and grasped Danny's right hand.

'I'm fine now, Danny,' Mick said. 'I just had a bit of bad news today. You know my old pal, Archie Reagan, who emigrated to Boston years ago?' asked Mick.

Danny nodded. He knew well whom Mick was talking about. Archie was Mick's best pal, in fact he was his best man at his wedding, and Mick always kept in touch with him after he left Ireland, so Danny felt that, although he was only a baby when Archie left, he kind of knew him well, too.

Mick continued. 'You know then that myself and Archie were very close and still are, even though we haven't seen each other in ten years.'

Danny nodded again. He was nervous about what was so bad that it had upset his father so much.

'Is he dead?' Danny blurted out.

Mick smiled, but it was an uncomfortable smile. 'No son. He's not dead. Sorry, son, I'm finding this a bit difficult.'

'It's alright, Da,' said Danny. 'What is it?'

Mick went on to tell Danny that Archie's youngest daughter, Clara, was very ill. She had been diagnosed with cancer in her right arm. Archie had rang Mick earlier that day and was devastated on the phone. This had really upset Mick and had left him a little shaken.

'Is she going to be alright, Da?' Danny asked.

'I think so, son,' Mick said. 'She has to have a big operation soon. I think she'll be fine after that.'

Mick explained to Danny that the GAA club that Archie was involved with in Boston – Boston Blues – was going to have a big fund raising day in November to help fund Clara's operation.

'That's animal, Da,' said Danny. 'You can't beat the GAA. Isn't that right?'

'That's right, son.' Mick smiled. 'We're a family, and we look after each other. Don't ever forget that, son. Did I mention that Clara plays for their girls' under-fourteen's team?'

'No way!' said Danny.

Mick nodded. 'According to Archie, she's captain of the team, and a good player, Danny.'

Danny brought Mick's empty dishes over to the kitchen sink, and then turned back around to Mick.

'She has to get that operation, Da,' said Danny.

'I know, son,' Mick said.

'We can help. We could do some fund raising here for her. After all, we're all one big family in the GAA. You said it yourself.'

Mick was proud of Danny's suggestion, and went straight to work with Danny on ideas of how they and the team were going to help Clara.

Chapter Five

Team Meeting

By the time Tuesday night's training came along, Danny and Mick had all their plans worked out to raise funds for Clara.

As Jimmy was setting up some cones for sprints, Mick called all of his players into a circle.

He had already discussed everything with Jimmy and had his full support.

'Before we get started lads, I want to fill yiz all in on some news and I want all your help.'

All of Mick's players listened carefully.

Jimmy joined the group and nodded to Mick as if to say, *In your own time coach!*

'Right,' Mick started. 'Um! Well! I suppose to make a long story short, um ...'

Danny could sense that his dad was struggling a bit. It wasn't like Mick to struggle when speaking to his own players.

Danny wanted to jump in and help his dad like he had done on more than one occasion for Jimmy when Mick wasn't present, but he didn't. He knew his dad would pull it together in front of his players.

Suddenly Mick found courage.

'Look, lads, what I have to ask of yiz is very important to me. A friend of mine's daughter – she's about your age – is ill and she needs a big operation.'

That was the hard part out of the way, and the rest flowed with ease as Mick told his players all about Clara and how she was a GAA player just like them and he wanted his team to rally together to raise funds.

'So, everyone's up for a night of bag packing at Tesco on Thursday night instead of training?' asked Mick.

Mick got a great response. Everyone

expressed great enthusiasm to help out.

'Good lads,' added Jimmy. 'Right. Will we do a spot of training, Mick?'

Mick gave Jimmy the thumbs up, but then as Jimmy was calling everyone over to the cones he had a change of plan.

'I think we'll give the sprints a miss tonight Jimmy,' suggested Mick. 'Why don't we have a bit of fun.'

'Nice one, Coach,' cheered Paddy Timmons, Crokes right full back. 'Are you taking us down to the Fun Fair? It opened last night.'

Mick laughed. *Fair play to ya' Paddy, ya' chancer!* he thought.

'I was thinking more along the lines of a game of frozen ball,' Mick said.

Danny jumped on the spot and punched the air.

'Savage!'

Jonathon didn't share his cousin's enthusiasm. He remembered the last time they played frozen ball in training and Mick wasn't present.

Danny had convinced Jimmy that it would be a good idea to kick the ball at the frozen players instead of fisting it.

Jonathon could almost still feel the burning sensation in his left ear from Danny's lethal hook around Big Johnner Purcell's head as Danny picked out Jonathon for teasing him.

'Can we kick instead of fisting?' pleaded Danny.

'No!' answered Mick and Jimmy together. Jimmy had confessed all to Mick.

The two coaches laughed.

Jimmy re-arranged the cones and set up a playing area about half the size of a basketball court. He had made a square using the cones.

The object of frozen ball was that all players start the game with three lives.

The coach – Jimmy in this instance – would randomly pick a player by calling his name out. He would then throw the ball up in the air. The player named would run to catch the ball while the others scattered. The named player then, after catching the ball, would call out 'Freeze'. All the other players would then stand still.

The named player would then fist the ball in the direction of the player nearest to him, and if hit, that player would lose a life.

The player who had just lost a life would then continue the game from the centre of the playing area, and so on.

Mick added his own little twist to the game – a forfeit!

The first player to lose his three lives would have to do a forfeit, chosen by the player who had fisted the last ball at him. All within reason of course, but the last time they played frozen ball Splinter had made Paddy Timmons dance like a ballerina, all the way around the outside of the park – twice!

Jimmy threw the ball in the air and called out the first name – Barry Sweeney. The game had begun, and everyone scattered.

After about half an hour, about half the players were on their last life – Todd included.

Danny had just lost his second life, and when he called out, 'Freeze!' Todd Bailey was the nearest player to him.

Danny grinned at Todd – a real cheeky grin, as he fisted the ball long and hard, bouncing it off Todd's left shoulder.

Danny knew exactly what Todd's forfeit would be; everyone burst out laughing as he announced it.

'No way, mate,' said Todd. 'Rack off! I'm not going to your uncle's Halloween party dressed like *that*!'

Mick and Jimmy piled on the pressure.

'You have to do the forfeit, Todd,' said Mick. 'Isn't that right, Jimmy?'

'That's right, Mick,' Jimmy said, trying his best to hold a serious face. 'Honour,' added Jimmy. 'A fine attribute of GAA.'

Everyone gave Todd a fair bit of stick for a few minutes until they all forgot about it as soon as Jimmy set up two goals for a short friendly match. But Danny, Splinter and Jonathon were all determined to remind Todd of his forfeit before Larry's party at Halloween!

Chapter Six

Fundraising!

The rain was hammering down on the roof of Tesco on Thursday night, but it didn't stop the shop from being jam-packed. It was the busiest night for shopping, and Mick knew that. He also knew that Jimmy's wife, Ann, was assistant floor manager and that she wouldn't hesitate to support them, even at such short notice.

At every till there was a Crokes' player with a bucket that Jimmy had supplied them with. Jimmy worked in a hardware warehouse and his boss was only too glad to give him the new buckets, after he explained to him what they were for.

Danny and Jonathon were bag packing together, with Todd on one side and Splinter and little John Watson on the other.

Mick and Jimmy were centred between the tills with a bucket each.

Todd had his head down, packing away, when the old lady whose bags he was packing, put her hand on his arm.

Todd looked up. He hadn't noticed that the woman was his next-door neighbour on Clifford Road.

'Aw, hi, Mrs. Duff. I didn't notice ya there.'

'I hear you're going back to Australia,' announced the old woman. Her hearing was partially impaired so she had a tendency to speak very loudly.

Everyone on every till heard her.

Todd looked straight to Danny, who by now was looking over at Mick and Jimmy, thinking, *Is she for real?*

Todd went red.

'I'm going to miss yiz terrible,' said the old woman. 'Yiz were lovely neighbours.'

'Thanks,' said Todd, who looked mortified; this wasn't the way he'd wanted to break the news.

The old woman bid him farewell, and went out of the shop leaving nothing but total devastation behind.

Danny thought his dad and Jimmy would have shot straight over to quiz Todd on this revelation, but they didn't. This information had come out unexpectedly and Mick knew how embarrassed Todd was.

But Mick wasn't a teenager like Splinter.

'Is that true Todd?' asked Splinter, his jaw almost on the floor.

Todd nodded.

'When?' asked Danny.

'Next week,' said Todd.

'Next week,' repeated Danny. 'When were you going to tell us?'

The tension was building between the boys.

'You better get in there, Mick,' Jimmy advised.

Mick casually made his way over to Todd's till.

'Leave it, Danny,' warned Mick. 'This isn't

the time nor the place.'

'Sorry Danny, mate,' said Todd. 'We only decided last night. Mum was going into school tomorrow, and I was gonna tell everyone then.'

'That's okay, Todd,' Mick said, but deep down, he was gutted.

'Why are you leaving, Todd?' asked Jonathon.

'Yeah! Do ya not like it here?' asked Splinter.

'Shut up, Splinter,' said Danny.

Todd gave Danny a smile that seemed to say, *Thanks, mate.*

Just as Todd was about to explain everything, Mick noticed Sarah – Todd's mother – waving at him from the tinned beans and peas aisle.

She was calling him over.

'Back in a second, lads,' said Mick.

'Hi, Mick,' Sarah greeted him. She had seen Mrs Duff talking to Todd a few minutes earlier, and knew that the old woman must have said something.

'Hi, Sarah,' Mick said. 'Doing a bit of

shopping?' Mick was very fond of Sarah and always got a little boyish around her.

'Oh, yeah,' Sarah said back. 'Um, Mick. Did Todd mention our news to you?'

'What news?' asked Mick playfully. 'Would that be the news that the old biddy just announced to the whole shop?' Mick laughed.

Sarah blushed.

'Sorry, Mick. We were going to tell everyone tomorrow.'

Mick could see that Sarah was embarrassed. He patted her on the arm.

'It's fine, Sarah. When are yiz off?' He was trying to be as brave as he could. Deep down he dreaded the thought of Sarah returning to Australia.

'Saturday week, the seventh of November, I think.'

'Jaysis! That wasn't much notice,' said Mick with a smile.

'Sorry, Mick.'

'Oh! God, no. I didn't mean it like that. I

meant, it's all a bit sudden like. Not that that matters. I mean it does matter, of course. We'll miss yiz, of course.'

Sarah raised her eyebrows.

'Really?'

Now Mick was embarrassed.

'Yeah! Of course. I mean, Todd's a great player. The team will be lost without him.'

'Do you remember helping me on this aisle, the time I knocked over all the tins?' asked Sarah.

'I do.'

Sarah put her hand on Mick's shoulder.

'Thanks, Mick. You and Danny and every-one at the club have been very kind to Todd and me. We'll really miss you all.'

Mick could feel a lump in his throat.

'Yiz don't have to go,' he said.

'Todd's been missing home and I suppose I have too.'

Suddenly, a loud cheer erupted from the tills.

'I think you might be needed over there,'

Sarah said. She could see Jimmy trying to call order.

Mick gave Sarah a friendly wink, and wished her luck, then joined the others.

* * *

It didn't take Danny very long to get over the shock of Todd's news and remember the reason for their bag-packing.

Tommy Dempsey – father of Sean 'Dirty' Dempsey, the player that Mick had kicked off his team last year – had infuriated Danny by refusing to put a donation into the bucket after Danny had packed his shopping.

'I wouldn't be caught dead putting money into Littlestown Crokes,' Dempsey protested. He hadn't even bothered to take the time to look at the 'Help Clara Fund' label that Danny and Mick had stuck to the buckets.

Danny was very upset.

'It's not for the club,' said Danny, holding up his bucket, almost to Dempsey's face.

Tommy Dempsey rolled his eyes at the label, and then lowered his face in shame.

He then took out all of his money from his pocket – a twenty-euro note and a twenty-cent coin. Dempsey put the twenty-cent coin in the bucket.

Danny was raging, but he had to be thankful for every donation.

'Thanks,' Danny said.

Tommy could feel the contempt coming towards him from everyone around. He looked down at the twenty-euro note in his hand.

'I'll tell you what, Wilde,' Dempsey said. 'If you finish ahead of us in the league, I'll give you this twenty euro for your collection.'

Danny's hand lunged forward. 'You're on.'

Tommy Dempsey didn't shake Danny's hand. He just nodded, grabbed his shopping and hurried off as he noticed Mick Wilde coming his way.

Chapter Seven

Clara

The fundraiser in Tesco was a huge success, and even though Mick was very proud of Danny and what he was doing for Clara, he still scolded him when they got home for getting involved with Tommy Dempsey.

'I'll have his twenty euro, Da,' Danny insisted.

Mick was at the computer.

'He's bad news Danny,' Mick said. 'You know what Tommy is like.'

'I don't care, Da. It's for the fund. It's for Clara. That's what matters.'

Mick turned around to Danny with a smile on his face.

'What?' Danny asked.

'There's an e-mail for you.'

'For me? I don't get e-mails. Who'd send me

an e-mail? Open it up, Da!'

Danny peered over Mick's shoulder.

'It's from Clara,' Mick said.

'Clara!'

Mick told Danny that he had sent Archie an e-mail the night before, telling him all about Danny's idea to raise funds for Clara's operation. Archie was so thrilled that he rang Mick to thank him and tell him about how happy it had made Clara and how she wanted Danny's e-mail address so she could thank Danny herself. Mick had forgotten to mention it to Danny.

'What does she want?' asked Danny.

'I don't know,' Mick said. 'Maybe she wants to thank you. Here, sit down son and read it.'

Danny sat down while Mick gave him a bit of privacy and made himself a cup of tea.

It was Danny's first e-mail from a girl and he couldn't wait to read what she had to say.

He read:

Dear Danny,

Hi. It's Clara. I just wanted to say THANKS for what you're doing for me. It's really amazing that you and your team-mates are doing this. Dad said that you're going bag packing in your local food store. I hope it goes well!

God! This is unreal! I have so many things that I want to say but my mind is all mixed up. Okay! Clara, get a grip. Sorry! You're probably thinking by now that this girl is weird.

Okay! Let me start again. Dad told me that you're captain of your team, The Crokes. Is that right, Danny? That's cool! I'm captain of my team too and we play under-fourteens too. We're called the Boston Blues.

I heard that you guys won your league last season and you did really well in some big tournament this summer. Wow! That's so amazing! We haven't won anything yet, but I think maybe soon we will. We're getting better and better each season.

I'm a huge Dubs fan. I love the 'Blues'. It's in the blood. I get it from Dad, of course. We're always looking at their matches on the net! Bad luck against Kerry this year.

I hear that you want to play for the Dubs one day and that you already play for their junior team. I hope I got that right. Junior doesn't sound right! Sorry! I'm sure you'll be a superstar, Danny. You are to me already!

Anyway! Sorry for going on and on. I'm just so excited that you're helping me. Please say a huge thank you to all your team-mates and your dad, of course. My dad loves him. He's always talking about him and how great he is and all about their GAA days together before we left for Boston.

Here I go again, on and on. Sorry, Danny. I'll go now.

I'd love to hear from you and all about your GAA team and stuff?

Bye for now,
Clara

Danny was gobsmacked.

Mick peered around the kitchen door.

'Everything okay, son?'

Mick was dying to know what Clara had to say in her e-mail to Danny, but this was Danny's business and he felt that he should give him some privacy and not ask him out straight.

Danny turned around to Mick.

'She's wired!'

Mick laughed.

'What do you mean, son?'

'She's just wired – mad. You know, like!'

'What did she have to say?' asked Mick. 'Did she just want to thank you?'

'Yeah! And about a hundred other things as well. Here, have a read, Da. She's a mad Dubs' fan.'

'I'm not surprised Danny,' said Mick. 'She's Archie's daughter. Are you going to reply to her?'

Danny looked up at Mick who was now leaning over him, glancing over the e-mail.

'She sounds lovely, Danny. You have to e-mail her back. Sure yiz have something in common already with the football, and you're both captains of your teams.'

Danny was uncomfortable.

'What?' asked Mick.

'But –' stuttered Danny.

'But what?'

'I don't know what to write. You know like, Da. I'm afraid that I might write the wrong thing, like with her not being well and that.'

Mick laughed.

'Then don't mention it, son. She sounded real upbeat in her e-mail. She sounds like a fighter Danny, just like you.'

Mick pulled a chair over beside Danny.

'I never told you this before, but when your mammy was sick – very sick – she used to say to people, *Cheer up! I'm not dying with cancer; I'm living with it!* Your mammy was just like Clara. Bubbly and happy and always thinking about the good things in her life, son and not worry-ing too much about the rest.'

Danny loved when his dad talked about his

mam, even if it made him a little sad, he didn't mind. It was special when his dad shared memories with him.

'Do you think that Clara will be okay, Da?' asked Danny. 'She won't die like Mam, will she?'

Mick put his arm around his son.

'She'll be fine, Danny. Mammy was a lot sicker than Clara, and it was a long time ago. Doctors can do wonderful things now. I'm sure once she has this operation, she'll be brand new.'

Danny felt a bit better.

'I'm going to reply to her,' he said.

'Good man.'

Danny's email to Clara said:

How ya, Clara?

It's Danny – Danny Wilde. I got your e-mail. Thanks. We did our collection in Tesco tonight. That's our local supermarket. Do you have any Tescos in America? Anyway! It went animal. Animal

means savage, in case you're wondering. Sorry!
Savage means deadly, I mean good – really good.
Sorry! That's the way we talk here. Well! Most of us.

Anyway! Oh yeah, the bag packing. Complete
success. We made loads of money. I'm not sure how
much yet cos my da hasn't counted it yet, but I will let
you know soon. Oh! And there's this ol' fella, Tommy
Dempsey. His son used to play for us last year but my
da kicked him off the team cos he was a nutter.
Anyway, his da – Tommy that is – put a bet on with
me for twenty euro. (We use euro in Ireland) that we
wouldn't finish above Barnfield. Barnfield is the
team that his son, Sean, plays for now. Shower of
muppets. Muppet means, well I don't know what
muppet means. I think it has something to do with
The Muppet Show. So, just imagine a load of mup-
pets in jerseys. That's Barnfield.

Anyway, we beat Barnfield in the last game of the
league last year to win the title and we beat them this
year in the semi-final of the Féile too.

The Féile was the tournament that you mentioned.
We didn't win it, but we gave it our best shot. One of

our best players, Todd, an Australian guy, was missing for the first half. I think we would have beaten Chapel Hall if Todd was playing for the whole match. He's going home next week. Can't believe it. Totally out of the blue!

Anyway, Barnfield. If we finish ahead of them, Tommy's going to have to hand over his twenty euro. Don't worry, Clara. I'm going to make him eat his words.

I think it's savage that you're captain of your team too. Hard work, isn't it?

But it's worth it!

I have to go now cos it's getting late. I think we might do another collection for you soon. I have to check with my da but I'm sure he said something to Jimmy about doing another one. Oh! Jimmy's our assistant coach. He's sound!

Danny

P.S. Happy Halloween. I'm going to a big party in my Uncle Larry's. Hope you have a great Halloween night on Saturday!

Chapter Eight

The Halloween Party

It was October 31, Halloween night, and an unsuspecting Garda sitting on his motor bike at a red light couldn't believe his eyes when Mick Wilde's car pulled up beside him.

The Garda lifted his black visor to reveal his laughing face.

Who could blame him – sitting in the front of the car were Mick and Jimmy dressed as Batman and Robin, with Danny in the back dressed as Wolverine, Splinter dressed as a Rubik's Cube and his mother, Ann, dressed as Morticia Addams.

The Garda leaned over and tapped on Jimmy's window.

'All right, Garda?' Jimmy asked; he sounded nervous.

The Garda took a few seconds to calm down before saying, 'Everything's just fine, lads. Well, now that I know that Batman and Robin are out on patrol. Keep up the good work gentlemen and try and leave a few villains for me, won't ya?'

The light changed green and the Garda sped off.

When Superheroes and Co. arrived at Larry's house, Jimmy and Ann seemed amazed at its size.

'Jaysis!' Jimmy gasped as Mick's car pulled up outside.

'It's a mansion!' Ann added.

'Would ya look at the set up here!' Mick said.

Larry had gone all out to make the Halloween party one to remember. He felt bad about the previous year's big upset at Halloween, when Jonathon and Danny sneaked off on a trip and got into trouble, and Larry had a big fight with Mick. Larry wanted to make it up to everyone this year.

There was no expense spared. Larry had hired an entertainment company to provide performers and actors dressed up in scary costumes. He even had the whole house decorated in a Halloween theme, and there was a tall, thin, hideous-looking man waiting at the gate to greet arrivals.

As Mick stopped his car at the gates, spooky music began to play as the electronic gates all covered in cobwebs screeched open. Mick rolled down his window as the tall man approached his car.

'Jeepers Creepers,' Mick said. 'Watch my back, Robin. I don't like the looks of this fella.'

Everyone laughed.

The tall man bent right over and stuck his head in Mick's open window. Mick leaned back into Jimmy.

'Get off me, Batman – I mean Mick,' Jimmy cried.

'Are you here for the party in the Haunted Mansion?' asked the man in a ghoulish voice.

'No,' Mick said. 'We heard there was a break-in so we thought we'd check it out.'

The creepy man's face was expressionless.

'Humour. How amusing.'

He stood upright and pointed his long finger toward a parking space in Larry's massive front driveway.

Danny elbowed Splinter with such excitement that he nearly burst through the box that Splinter had used to make the Rubik's Cube costume.

'Careful!' Splinter laughed.

'This is going to be savage, Splinter,' Danny said.

* * *

Larry's house was jam-packed. Work colleagues, neighbours, friends – there must have been over a hundred people all dressed in costume at the party.

Larry was dressed as Frankenstein; Regina, his wife, dressed as the bride of Frankenstein looked just as gruesome as Larry.

Jonathon spotted Danny and Splinter and

ran over to them.

'Splinter. You really puzzle me sometimes.'

Splinter stared back at Jonathon for a second, until he got the joke.

'What? Oh yeah! Good one, J!' Splinter laughed.

'Where's Todd?' asked Jonathon. He was dressed up as a pirate.

'He bailed out,' said Danny with a hint of disappointment in his voice.

'I don't blame him,' said Splinter. 'There was no way he was going to turn up here dressed up as Tinker Bell!'

The three pals burst out laughing.

'Hey, Danny,' Jonathon said. 'There's Trinity over there. Why don't you go and talk to her? You haven't seen her since the Féile.'

'I don't see her,' said Danny.

'She's in a costume,' Jonathon said. 'Look! The mummy.'

'I thought that mummy looked hot!' said Splinter.

'That doesn't make any sense, Splinter,' said Danny.

Splinter got a bit embarrassed. What he was really thinking was that the mummy had a figure that was *way* too good looking to be a boy's.

'Go on, Danny,' Jonathon nudged him. 'She won't be able to resist your Wolverine charms.'

'I might just go over and say hello,' Danny said in a kind of an *I'm not too bothered either way!* kind of tone, but deep down, he was dying to go over to speak to Trinity.

As Danny wrestled through the crowd, he lost sight of Trinity. He turned around sharply to Splinter and Jonathon with his arms raised. Splinter and Jonathon stood on their heels to see if they could find where she had gone.

Splinter pointed towards the kitchen door.

Danny gave Splinter a thumbs-up and headed in that direction.

There were just as many guests in the kitchen as in the hallway. Danny could see Trinity going out the back door into the garden, so he followed. She was heading across the first garden, toward the second garden where the tennis court was.

Trinity loves tennis, Danny thought. *She must be going down to the tennis court. I'll follow. We'll be alone. I can say what I really want to say without worrying about anyone hearing.*

Danny ran across the circular lawn of the second garden and through the rose arch where he found Trinity sitting on a rock in front of the tennis court.

He sat down beside her.

'Hi!'

Trinity didn't reply. She just nodded.

Probably can't speak with all those bandages wrapped around her face, Danny thought. *That's good. It'll give me a chance to say what I want to say.*

'I want to tell you something,' he began. He was very nervous. His mouth was dry and his voice was weak. 'I know that I went off the head a bit in the summer thinking that you and Todd were going out together, but that was because you went to the pictures with him and it made me jealous.'

He stopped there for a few seconds, waiting for some kind of reply from Trinity.

Trinity just nodded her head to gesture, *Go on.*

Danny continued, 'It was only because I like you so much. I mean like, a lot. Todd told me that you talked a lot about me when yiz went to the pictures. Is that because you like me a lot too?'

Trinity nodded.

Danny drew breath. He felt like he hadn't breathed in any air since the first words that came out of his mouth. His face returned to its natural colour.

'That's animal!' he smiled. *Ah! What did I say that for? That was stupid. I have to get this right. Ah! What the hell! Just go for it, Danny.*

Then without wasting another second, Danny Wilde did what he wanted to do for a long time and asked Trinity to be his girlfriend.

Trinity started to remove the bandages from her face.

I'm going to get a kiss! he thought.

Slowly she removed the bandages, revealing her face … and said, 'I only came out here for some peace. I've a thumping headache.'

'*You're* not Trinity!' Danny squealed, shocked.

Sitting in front of him with a smile on her face as wide as Larry's gates was Jonathon's seventeen-year-old cousin, Avril.

Avril was related to Jonathon on his mum's side of the family, and Jonathon despised her for her nastiness.

Danny jumped up in horror. 'I'm sorry. I thought you were someone else.'

'Apparently. Wait until Trinity Dawson hears this. I can't *wait* to tell her.'

Danny was mortified. He had just expressed his feelings for Trinity for the first time and to his complete horror, it wasn't even to Trinity!

Aw, man! he thought. *That was one of the hardest things I've ever done and it was all for nothing. Now I'm going to look like a proper muppet when she tells Trinity.*

* * *

After Danny scolded Splinter for sending him off chasing the wrong mummy, he spent pretty much of the rest of the night avoiding the right mummy – Trinity – who by now had probably been told everything that Danny had wanted her to hear from him.

But he couldn't avoid her forever, and before the night was over, she finally caught up with him when the two of them were selected to team up together in a Halloween game.

Regina had been organising games all night and this was to be the last one.

There were ten couples, selected by pulling names out of a hat. Each couple had to be bound together with ribbon, and when Regina decided that everybody had enough ribbon around them she blew a whistle.

The ten couples then had to try to make their way out into the back gardens and find the treasure that Regina and Larry had hid earlier that evening. It was hilarious. Everybody really struggled to get where they wanted to go because the ribbons made it so hard to walk.

Danny had protested when he was initially chosen to take part in the game, but now he was kind of glad. He was close to Trinity, maybe too close, but closer than ever before.

Ten minutes had passed and four out of the five treasures had been found.

'Over this way, Danny,' Trinity whispered in his ear.

Trinity carefully steered Danny beyond the cobbled circle with the water fountain of the boy and girl holding an umbrella. The couple shuffled their way to the end of the first garden where a cluster of neatly clipped bay bushes gathered beneath a tall silver birch tree.

'In there,' said Trinity. 'I knew I could see

something glittering.'

Tucked behind one of the bays with a spotlight reflecting off its gleaming red wrapping was the last treasure.

'How are we going to pick it up?' Danny asked.

They hunkered down and Danny stretched out his fingers and grasped the treasure.

'Come on,' said Danny. 'Let's tell the others we found the last one. I wonder what it is …'

Danny was just about to move when Trinity held back.

'Wait a second, Danny.'

Danny felt his stomach turn, dreading what Trinity had to say next.

'I'm sorry that Avril did that to you earlier. That was bad.'

Relief washed over Danny. He thought that Trinity was going to go berserk!

'It's all right.' He shrugged. 'Um, did she say much?'

'Everything.'

Danny went scarlet.

'I really like you too, Danny.' She gave him a smile.

Danny's eyes widened. 'Really?'

Trinity nodded. Danny went weak at the knees. This was exactly what he had wished for.

But just as she moved her face in closer to Danny's, Splinter let an unmerciful roar. 'Danny and Trinity found the last treasure.'

* * *

Uncle Larry's Halloween party was over. The last thing to do was to untie all the couples that had taken part in the treasure hunt and reveal their prizes.

'Here, Trinity,' Danny said, once their parcel was opened, 'You can have it.'

'What did yiz get?' asked Mick.

Trinity smiled. 'Free passes into the fun fair and fifty euro worth of tokens.'

'Nice one, Trinity,' Lowry, Jonathon's sister and Trinity's best friend, congratulated her.

'When are we going?'

'*You're* not!' said Larry. 'That prize is a couple's prize. She has to take Danny.'

'*Wooooo*!' everyone cheered.

Trinity and Danny were embarrassed, but thanks to Larry, their first date was arranged.

* * *

Splinter went into school on the Monday morning after Larry's party and told everyone all about Trinity. Danny was the centre of attention in his class.

'What's she look like?'

'How old is she? She's older than you!'

'Splinter says she's dead fit!'

'I heard she blew out Todd for you!'

'When are you meeting up with her?'

Danny had to put up with questions all week long. Splinter did most of the answering, which seemed fitting considering it was Splinter who started it all.

Splinter described Trinity as tall and slim

with long blonde hair and 'savage' blue eyes, but most importantly to Splinter was the fact that Trinity was older. *That* was something to brag about.

'I'd be bragging if she was my bird!' Splinter said with a smile.

That got the biggest laugh from Danny, but by the time Saturday came along, Danny was looking forward to the distraction of a football match.

Chapter Nine

Fergally G.F.C v Littlestown Crokes

It was 7 November, the morning of Littlestown Crokes' second-last league game in the under-Fourteen's Division 1.

Danny's team had struggled in the first half of the season, but gained tremendous confidence from their super run in the Féile, reaching the final.

The Crokes had battled their way into contention for runner up spot in the league.

The top of their table looked like this with just two games remaining:

TEAM	PLAYED	WON	LOST	DRAW	POINTS
Chapel Hall	12	11	0	1	23
Barnfield	12	7	3	2	16
Littlestown Crokes	12	6	3	3	15

Chapel Hall were already league winners. There was no catching them and with all credit to Mick's team, the Crokes were the only team in the league to take a single point from them.

Barnfield were at home to Darnville, who were mid-table, and the Crokes were away to Fergally G.F.C., who were at the bottom.

They both were huge games for the Crokes and Barnfield as both were drawn yet again to play each other in the last game of the league on the Little Croker.

Everyone knew that the Crokes had the easier second-last game as Fergally were a poor side, but Barnfield were a point ahead of the Crokes in the league and this was playing on Danny's mind in the car on the way out to

Fergally's grounds.

'Do you think Barnfield will win today, Da?' Danny asked.

Todd was in the back of the car. He was flying out later that night to Australia, but had promised that he would play one more game for the Crokes.

'Aren't they ahead of us in the league?' Todd responded first.

'That's right, Todd,' Mick agreed. 'It's out of our hands, Danny. Don't even think about it, son. All we can do is play our game and hope that Darnville do us a favour today by beating Barnfield.'

'Unlikely!' huffed Danny, who was thinking about Tommy Dempsey's taunting words in Tesco, the night that they were fund raising for Clara.

If you finish ahead of us in the league, I'll give you this twenty euro for your collection.

* * *

Mick pulled Barry Sweeney and Doyler to one

side before he announced his team to play Fergally.

Barry Sweeney had lost his position in the team when he broke his collarbone earlier in the season in the game against Chapel Hall on the Little Croker.

Mick had pushed Doyler up into Barry's full forward position and Todd had then joined the team and taken up the position of centre half forward.

Both Todd and Doyler played well for the rest of the season and Barry struggled to get back into the starting fifteen.

This was something that Mick, along with every other good coach, had to face when selecting a team.

'Right lads,' Mick started, 'as yiz both know, this is Todd's last game before he goes home.'

Barry and Doyler nodded their heads in anticipation of Mick's next words.

'I'm going to start you today, Barry,' Mick continued.

Barry's face lit up, but Doyler lowered his head in disappointment.

Mick put his hand on Doyler's shoulder.

'Don't worry, Doyler. I just want Barry to get a full game in before we play Barnfield in the last match. You'll be taking up your old position of centre half forward for that game. Is that alright, son?'

Doyler nodded and smiled. He was gutted, but he knew that Mick was just trying to do the right thing to get the right result for the whole team and sometimes that meant individuals making sacrifices.

* * *

Danny and Jonathon took up their positions in midfield as the referee called for everyone's attention.

'Best of luck Danny,' Jonathon said. He was his captain's rock.

Danny smiled back to his cousin.

'Let's make this a good one for Todd.'

He gave Todd a thumbs up. Todd winked and returned the gesture.

The whistle was blown and the ball was thrown in.

Danny was far superior to his opponent. He palmed the ball to Jonathon with ease and received a quick return to send him off on a Danny Wilde solo.

He dodged two players, then a third, before releasing a long ball out to Splinter at left full forward.

Splinter beat his marker to the ball and sent in a low and accurate pass along the ground to Barry.

Barry Sweeney clipped the ball up into his hands and instead of doing what he did best and knocking the ball over his head for a point, Barry unselfishly fisted the ball out to Todd who took aim and put Crokes ahead with a high kick between the posts.

Danny never took any game or opponent for granted, but he knew that this game was not going to be their toughest – they had already trashed Fergally on the Little Croker in their home game.

Danny could even hear one or two of the Fergally players whispering comments about him as he jogged back into position.

'He's a class player,' said one player.

'Yeah! He plays for the Dublin development squad. I heard that he's one of their best players – a future Dubs' player!' said another.

It felt great to Danny to hear other players talking about him like that, but he still had to knuckle in and get the result. That's what counted – not compliments on the field, but action – good action.

Danny didn't disappoint those two players. He turned on a performance that was by far one of the best individual performances of the season.

He scored three super points – set up Barry and Jason Delaney, Crokes' right full forward for a goal each and literally ran himself ragged in the first half.

By half time, nearly all the Fergally squad was talking about him – coaches and supporters included.

Crokes ran over for their half time oranges leading by a score of 0-0, 2-4.

Mick didn't have to think too hard as to what to say to his team at half time.

He was thrilled with their work rate and very proud of Danny, but he didn't say too much and over emphasize that, being Danny's dad as well as team coach.

Jimmy called Mick aside and suggested that he might make a couple of changes considering the Crokes were winning so easily. Mick agreed.

He replaced Brian O'Reilly at left half forward with little John Watson and Paddy Timmons at right full back with Niall Clarke.

Splinter made a slagging gesture to Paddy Timmons, which didn't go unnoticed by his father, Jimmy.

'Do you want to spend the second half in the car?' Jimmy asked, sternly. Neither Jimmy nor Mick tolerated any teasing of that kind.

'What?' Splinter laughed, then he realised that Jimmy was serious, so he hid in behind Todd, who was much bigger than him.

* * *

The second half was ten minutes under way when Jimmy's phone started ringing.

The Crokes had already added another three points. They were well on their way to slaughtering Fergally.

'You're kidding me,' Jimmy said into the phone.

That caught Mick's attention. He had a good hunch about who was on the other line.

Jimmy had asked his eldest son, Mark, to keep an eye on Barnfield's game against Darnville, as Barnfield's grounds weren't far from the Little Croker.

'Is that Mark?' Mick asked anxiously, while

trying to keep one eye on the game.

'Hold on, Mark,' said Jimmy. 'You're not going to believe it,' he said to Mick.

'What? Tell me!'

'Barnfield are five points down to Darnville.'

'Yes!' Mick cheered; he punched the air and spun around.

'Come on, Crokes,' Mick fussed. It was like a dream. 'How long left Jimmy?'

Jimmy didn't answer. He was all ears to whatever Mark was telling him.

'Okay! Thanks son. Ring me when it's over.' Jimmy put the phone back in his pocket. 'You're not going to believe this either, Mick.'

'What?'

Jimmy went on to tell Mick that Barnfield's manager had taken ill during the game.

'A stomach bug,' he said. 'The assistant manager was away, so Tommy Dempsey stepped in to manage the team for the rest of the game.'

'Mark says that he's causing uproar,' Jimmy said.

'He would,' Mick agreed.

Suddenly, Jimmy jumped up and cheered.

'Goal!'

Danny had buried a twenty-yard right hook into the back of Fergally's net.

Shortly afterwards, the referee blew the full time whistle, after Danny and Barry had added another point each.

The Crokes had beaten their deflated opponents by a score of 0-1 to 3-9.

Mick gathered all of his players together before everyone went back to their own cars for the journey home – he had the result of the Barnfield game! He and Jimmy were smiling as they announced to the team that Darnville had beaten Barnfield.

Everyone cheered.

'We only need to draw the last game,' said Mick.

Everyone was hyper going home. They honestly thought that Barnfield would be going into the last game of the season with the upper hand on Crokes, but Darnville did them the favour they wished for and now Crokes were in the runner up spot going into the final game on the Little Croker on 21 November.

Chapter Ten

An Email From Clara

Mick and Danny dropped Todd to his house on the way home.

Mick wanted to say a proper goodbye to Sarah and he knew that Danny and Todd probably wanted to say their goodbyes too. They had become good friends over the past seven months.

Sarah had noticed the car pulling up outside. She came out to greet them.

Todd grabbed his bag out of the boot of Mick's car and put his hand out to shake Danny's.

Danny grasped Todd's hand and the two pals gave each other a boyish hug and a pat on the back.

Mick and Sarah just shook hands.

'Text me,' Danny said to Todd.

'No problem, mate. I'll fill ya in on all my footy, that's if I can remember how to play footy.'

'I'm sure your mate, Wayne, will help you remember a thing or two.' Danny smiled at him.

The two boys laughed.

They said their final goodbyes, and then Mick and Danny drove off down the road, leaving Todd and Sarah standing at their gate waving.

* * *

The following morning, Mick and Danny went to put flowers on Danny's mam's grave.

It was her anniversary – a sad day in their lives every year – but Danny and Mick drew great strength from each other's support.

The sun was radiant, and Mick and Danny were sitting on the grass. Mick was telling Danny different stories about his mam.

Danny felt that his mam was there with them

as he listened to his father, and watched carefully how his father's face lit up with each and every happy memory.

'Is there anything mammy really wanted to do but never got the chance to?' Danny asked.

Mick had to think for a few seconds.

Danny spoke again before Mick could answer because he suddenly realised that maybe the question would make his father think of how Danny's mam would really loved to have been around while Danny was growing up.

'Like, did she ever want to go anywhere, and didn't get the chance to?'

Mick smiled.

'America,' he said.

'Really?' Danny's eyes lit up. 'Why?'

Mick shrugged.

'Not sure, son. She just always seemed to want to go there – to see America. I don't know whether it was the size of the country or its history or maybe just the shops.' Mick laughed.

Danny laughed, too.

'It's a pity she didn't get to go, Da,' Danny said.

'I know, son,' said Mick. 'Some things in life are just not meant to be. Who knows, maybe some day we'll get to see it for her.'

'Yeah!' Danny smiled. Suddenly, he thought of his dream that he shared with his pals in the school toilets.

Just maybe, Da, he thought. *Just maybe!*

* * *

After dinner, Danny thought that he would check his e-mail to see if there was one from Clara.

There was, and it said:

Hi Danny,
Thanks for your e-mail. It was great to hear from you, or should I say 'savage'! I hope I got that right. You're so funny, Danny. I couldn't stop laughing after I read the piece about the Barnfield players being

muppets. *I couldn't get the funniest picture out of my head of Kermit the Frog playing in goal and Miss Piggy up full forward and Fuzzy bear and Gonzo and, well, I think you get the picture by now. The doctors say that it's good for me to laugh, so thanks.*

It was really super to read all about your team. I hope you do finish better than Barnfield. That Tommy guy sounds like a nasty piece of work.

How did your uncle's party go? I hope you had a good time! Did you wear a costume? I'm thinking now of what you might have dressed up as. Let me see! Well! I'm guessing something really cool, like an X-man or something like that. Am I right, Danny? You're probably going to tell me that was silly or something and you went to the party as a vampire. They're all the rage over here in the States.

We had a brilliant Halloween night. Dad let me have a few of my girlfriends over because I was feeling a little bit tired from my medication. We didn't go out or anything. We just watched scary movies in my room and ate way too much junk food.

Courtney stayed over. She's my best friend.

What's your best friend's name, Danny? I bet he's funny just like you.

That's really it for now. Gosh! That was a big 'thank you' e-mail! I'm a bit of a talker, or in this case, writer.

Before I go, I wanted to ask you something if that's okay? Well, it's not just me. Dad and mam and well, all the Reagan family were wondering, too.

Our club, Boston Blues, they're having a big fund-raiser for me at the end of the month. I think Dad mentioned it to Mick. Anyway, I was wondering, and the rest of the gang of course, if you and your dad would like to come over to Boston for that weekend. What do you think?

No problem if you don't want to or you can't make it. It's just that we'd love to have you guys here, and Dad and Mam would love to see Mick again. It's been so long.

Think about it. As I said, it's no problem if you can't make it.

Bye for now!

Clara

Danny jumped straight out of his chair and went looking for Mick. Mick was at the front door having a chat with Jimmy about the match the day before and how they were going to go into the final game against Barnfield.

'Da!' Danny called, excitedly.

'How ya, Danny?' Jimmy asked.

'All right, Jimmy.'

'What is it, son?' Mick asked. He could see that Danny had something good to tell him.

'You're not going to believe it, Da.'

Mick waited.

'Clara wants … I mean Archie, too. They all want us to go over to Boston for the fund raiser.'

'What?' Mick was shocked.

'That's great, lads,' said Jimmy. 'You two haven't had a holiday in ages. It'll do yiz the world of good.'

Jimmy knew it was Danny's mam's anniversary. That was partly the reason why he called over to see Mick. That was just the way Jimmy was, and

Mick loved that about him.

'Can we go, Da?' Danny asked.

Mick was still in shock. He couldn't help but think of how he and Danny had discussed earlier that day how Danny's mam would have loved to have gone to America, and now this was happening on her anniversary.

Maybe we'll get to see it for her! The memory of his own words spun around in Mick's head.

This was meant to be! he thought.

'Go on, Mick,' Jimmy encouraged.

Danny waited nervously for Mick's reply.

Finally, Mick spoke, 'Boston here we come!'

Danny and Mick danced around in a circle, while Jimmy patted them on the back, chuffed to bits to see them so happy.

Danny left Mick and Jimmy at the door and returned to the computer to let Clara know that they were coming to Boston.

He wrote:

How ya, Clara.

Guess what! We're coming over to Boston. I can't believe it. Thanks for asking. This is like a dream. In fact, I was only dreaming recently that me and my da were on a plane. This is animal! I can't wait to tell Splinter. Oh yeah, Splinter is my best friend. He's stone mad. The things he comes out with. If you think I'm funny, you'd crack up if you met Splinter.

Wait until you hear what he went dressed as to Larry's party – a Rubik's Cube – imagine that! You were bang on about me. I was Wolverine. He's my favourite character in films.

I'm glad you enjoyed Halloween. Courtney sounds like a good mate. We all need one good mate in life. That's something my da always says to me.

Anyways! My da is going to ring your da later and make plans. I think he's going to book the flights as well. Man! I can't believe this is happening.

Thanks again, Clara.

Danny

Chapter Eleven

At The Fun Fair

Jimmy was so happy for Mick that he persuaded him to go to the pub later that
evening with him for just the one pint. Danny
had already arranged with Trinity to go to the
fun fair, compliments of Larry and Regina's
treasure hunt.

It was six thirty and Danny was putting the
finishing touches to his hair.

Maybe I should put a bit more gel in! he thought.

The doorbell rang.

Danny ran down stairs. He could see Trinity's
shape through the beveled glass of the front
door. He started to get those butterflies in his
stomach again.

Get it together, Danny! he thought before he
finally opened the door.

Danny was gobsmacked – Trinity looked amazing!

There was a beep from the car outside the gates.

Trinity waved goodbye to her mother. She was all Danny's now, and that made him feel like he was on top of the world.

The fun fair was only a fifteen-minute walk from the house; Trinity could hardly get a word in with Danny. He was buzzing with excitement about his trip to Boston.

'That's so cool, Danny,' Trinity said.

'Have you ever been to Boston?' asked Danny.

'Twice.'

'Really? And there's me going on about it so much.'

'You'll love it, Danny.' Trinity smiled. 'There's so much to see and do. Last time, we were there for a week and still didn't have enough time to fit everything in.'

'We're only going for a weekend.'

'I'm sure you'll make the most of it. I think it's really great that your dad is going to see his old friend again,' she said.

Danny hadn't mentioned Clara. He just said that Mick's old friend, Archie, had invited them over. It wasn't because he was embarrassed or even that he didn't want Trinity to know anything about her. It was just that this was his first date with Trinity, and he felt that it wouldn't help his first date get off to a good start if he spoke of another girl.

* * *

The fun fair was teeming with people.

Trinity had the fifty euro-worth of tokens that they had won at Larry's party.

'Let's get on the big wheel,' Trinity said.

Danny wasn't great with heights. In fact, he was petrified of heights.

What was I thinking, coming here? thought Danny as he and Trinity stepped into the carriage of the big wheel.

As soon as the wheel began to move, Trinity noticed that Danny had paled.

'Are you okay, Danny?'

'Fine!' he replied, trying not to look down at the ground, even though they hadn't actually left the ground yet.

As the wheel rotated and Danny and Trinity began to rise into the dark starry night, Trinity tucked her left arm around Danny's right arm and pulled him in close to her.

Instantly, Danny felt better, although he didn't dare to look over the edge. His legs were like jelly when they finally got off the big wheel.

'I'm thinking that you didn't like that, Danny,' Trinity laughed.

'Me?' gasped Danny. 'That was savage!'

Trinity knew better, but she thought it was sweet that Danny was trying to act tough and not show his weakness.

Danny looked all around, praying that she wouldn't drag him onto something like that again.

'Let's go over to the Wild West counter,' he suggested. He dragged Trinity's arm swiftly into the safer zone of the fun fair.

'I'll win ya a teddy bear,' Danny said.

Trinity laughed.

Danny blushed. *That was stupid!* he thought. *She must think I'm a kid now after saying that.*

Trinity pointed to a pink elephant.

'I love that one.'

Danny perked up.

'What do I have to do?' he asked the man.

But just then, the man was called away by a woman down the other end. A young boy stepped in to answer Danny's question.

'Knock the five tins over and you win anything along the bottom row,' the boy replied.

Danny looked at him with a judgmental stare.

'How do I win the big ones up top?'

'You have to knock them all over with just one shot.'

'What?' said Danny. 'That's impossible!'

'No, it's not!'

'Yeah, it is.'

Trinity handed two tokens to the boy.

'Go on, Danny. You can do it.'

I'll show him! thought Danny as he took aim.

Danny aimed for the tin in the middle – dead centre.

BANG!

Two tins fell off.

'Hard luck.' The boy gave him a smirk. 'You have two more goes. You can still win a prize.'

Danny gave him the evil eye, and then took aim.

BANG!

The rest of the tins fell over.

Trinity gave Danny a hug.

'Well done!'

Danny was disappointed. His competitive side was coming out.

'Look!' Trinity smiled. 'I'm just as happy with this small pink elephant as the big one.'

Just as they turned to walk away, the boy made a remark under his breath.

'Should have gone to Specsavers!'

Danny turned around sharply.

'What did you say?'

'Come on, Danny,' urged Trinity. 'He's only a little boy!'

The boy winked at Trinity. He was a right little scoundrel.

With that, Trinity changed her mind.

'Actually, I'll have a go.'

Before she took her first shot, she made a suggestion to the boy.

'I'll make a deal with you, just to make this a little more interesting. If I knock all of the tins down with one shot, you give me the big pink elephant and my tokens back.'

'What's in it for me?' asked the boy.

'If I don't, then I'll give you ten tokens for yourself.'

The boy looked down the line. His parents weren't paying attention.

'You're on!'

Trinity took aim. Danny was amazed. This was a side to Trinity that he never saw before, but he liked it.

BANG!

Trinity shot the bottom right corner of the far tin to the left. All the tins scattered – every single one of them.

Danny cheered!

'Hand it over!' Danny said to the boy, a huge grin on his face.

'How did you do that?' Danny asked Trinity.

'Everything has a weak spot. You just have to find it. That and a whole lot of luck!'

Danny had spotted a football game over in the far corner of the fair, just to the right of the slingshot. There was a group of lads all gathered around, cheering and having lots of banter.

As Danny and Trinity approached, Danny noticed that it was Splinter and a few of his teammates.

Danny was just about to steer Trinity away when Alan Whelan saw him.

'Hey, there's Danny!'

Everyone turned around.

Ah, no! thought Danny.

'Aren't they on your team, Danny?' Trinity asked.

Danny gave Trinity a sort of look that said, *Yeah! Unfortunately.*

'All right, lads,' Danny greeted them.

'What's the story Danny?' asked little John Watson. 'Is that your bird? I love her pink elephant!'

Danny blushed. Trinity giggled. She knew Danny wasn't going to enjoy this, but it was kind of funny.

The crowd opened up and Danny could see who was taking shots on the electronic goal.

It was Sean 'Dirty' Dempsey and some of his friends, including Deco Savage.

'I hope you're not cheering for that muppet,' Danny said to Splinter.

'No, we're not Danny. We're having a contest – Crokes against Barnfield.'

'Who's winning?' Danny asked.

'They are,' interrupted Doyler.

Suddenly, Dempsey caught a glimpse of Danny. 'Look who's here. Wilde-boy and his girlfriend.'

All the Barnfield boys laughed.

Danny stepped forward. Trinity tried to grab his hand to hold him back – she knew all about the rivalry between Danny and Dempsey. Her brother, Sebastian, was in Jonathon's class and he was always hearing stories from Jonathon about Crokes and Barnfield.

'I am a Wilde boy, Dempsey,' Danny teased. 'And proud to be one.' Danny felt like his favourite character, Wolverine, confronting an evil adversary.

'Go on, Danny,' said little John Watson encouragingly.

'Your teammates are letting you down, Danny,' Dempsey said. 'We're beating them.

No! We're trashing them. You should get your da to teach them how to shoot.'

'Is that right?' Danny asked. 'I hear your da hasn't got a bog about managing a team. Nice result against Darnville yesterday, by the way. I hope your manager gets better for the game against us. That way yiz might have a chance – just a small, teensy one – not much more than your ability to shoot.'

Now all the Crokes' boys were cheering.

Dempsey looked furious.

Deco Savage couldn't take any more. He stepped up and grabbed the ball from Dempsey.

'You think you're all that in front of your girl-friend, don't ya, Wilde?'

Trinity was getting very twitchy. She wasn't used to seeing confrontation at this level.

'Don't worry, Trinity,' Splinter told her. 'It's only football – nothing sinister.'

Savage threw the ball to Danny.

'We're winning by three goals. I'll give yiz the

game if you can score in the top right corner.'
Savage then placed the ball on the floor.

'That's impossible,' Splinter told him. 'That's the hardest spot to hit!'

Danny thought long and hard.

'What's wrong, Danny?' Dempsey teased. 'Are you afraid of failing in front of your girl-friend?'

Danny looked at Trinity. He had forgotten about her for a moment or two while all the banter was going on. That's the effect football had on Danny. It was like it cast a spell over him.

Trinity looked lost and Danny felt bad that their date had turned into a football contest.

Danny threw the ball back to Savage and walked over to Trinity.

'Come on, Trinity.'

'Thought you might chicken out.'

Danny turned around.

'I'm not chicken, ya dope. I just don't want to look like a show off by making you look like a loser in front of all your buddies.'

Danny strolled off, biting his lower lip as Savage and Dempsey and the rest of the Barnfield players hurled a cackle of chicken sounds at him.

Splinter ran after Danny.

'Are ya going to let them slag ya' like that, Danny? Come on back. You can hit that spot.'

'It's not about that, Splinter,' said Danny.

'But we could beat them.'

'Sometimes you have to lose to win,' Trinity said.

Splinter looked at Trinity as if she had suddenly sprouted three heads.

'What?'

Danny tapped Splinter on the arm.

'Forget it, Splinter. We'll beat them when it matters – on the Little Croker.'

Trinity tugged on Danny's arm. She thought how grown up he was – almost heroic.

'Come on, you two. Let's get on the slingshot. It takes three.'

Danny sat in the middle with Trinity on his right and Splinter on his left, wondering if this was going to be the last time he would feel his feet touch the ground.

'This is animal! Nice one, Trinity!' Splinter said.

'Are yiz ready?' asked the man in charge.

Danny nodded. Trinity smiled. Splinter screamed,

'YEE- HAW! Hold onto your jocks!'

Suddenly, VROOOOOM! They were launched sky-high.

'Aaaaaaaaaaagh!' the three of them screamed.

Danny felt like his face was being sucked inside out.

They bobbled in the air a few times before slowly being lowered back to the ground.

'Man! That was class!' shouted Splinter. 'Yee--Haw!'

He begged Danny and Trinity to lend him the photo of the three of them as they were launched into the air. He ran off to find the others and show them.

Trinity noticed that the football game area was empty.

She dragged Danny over and handed a token to the girl at the counter.

Trinity picked up the ball and handed it to Danny.

'What?' Danny asked.

'I know you were dying to make that shot,' Trinity said. 'Go on then!'

Danny looked around at the goal, then he looked around to see if anyone was watching, then he looked at Trinity and placed the ball on the spot.

Danny took two steps back and another step to the left.

He took a deep breath then gently swerved the ball towards the goal.

Trinity watched with her hands clasped as the electronic goalkeeper dived for the ball, only to be beaten. The ball hit the spot in the top right corner, exactly what Danny had aimed for.

Trinity jumped up and down, and then gave Danny a big hug.

'I knew you could do it.'

Danny looked into Trinity Dawson's eyes, thinking, *It doesn't get any better than this!*

Chapter Twelve

Mick Helps Out

Tuesday night's training was extra hard.
Mick ran the legs off all his players.

'We have to be at our best for the Barnfield
game,' was what he kept saying.

Jimmy thought there was something the
matter with Mick – something on his mind.

He called Danny to one side while everyone
was having a breather.

'Is your daddy alright, Danny?' Jimmy
whispered.

'He got bad news in work,' replied Danny.

'I thought there was something wrong. I
haven't seen your daddy run that hard in training since before his stroke last year. He ought to
take it easy. What happened in work? He never
said anything to me.'

'He's been put on a three-day week, Jimmy. I

think he's worried that it's only a matter of time before his job goes altogether.'

'That's terrible,' said Jimmy. 'The construction trade is gone to the wall – flamin' recession.'

Danny noticed Mick looking over in their direction.

'You better not say I told you, Jimmy,' Danny said. 'You know my da. He'll probably tell you later when he gets a chance.'

'Of course, Danny. Good man!'

Mick got Jimmy to set up a small playing field within the cones. He hadn't realised that he had used up all of the training time on running and exercises. The lads were very tired.

Mick wasn't impressed with what he saw in the game.

'Come on lads,' Mick said. 'If this is what yiz play like against Barnfield, we don't have a chance of winning the game.'

Jimmy thought he'd have a quiet word with Mick.

'I think they're knackered!' said Jimmy.

'We've already gone over by twenty minutes.'

Mick looked at his watch.

'I didn't notice, Jimmy. None the less, we'll let them play a bit longer. Practice makes perfect!'

Jimmy looked at Mick's strained face.

'Come on, Barry,' Mick said. 'Don't make me ring Todd in Australia and ask him to come back.'

Barry's head dropped.

'Let's call it a night, Mick,' Jimmy suggested. 'You're only getting frustrated with the boys. Danny told me about the job. I hounded him to tell me. I knew there was something on your mind.'

'Sorry, Jimmy,' Mick said. 'Is it that obvious?'

Jimmy nodded.

'All right, lads!' Mick yelled. Then he blew hard on his whistle. 'Go on, off yiz go. Well done, lads. I'm sorry for giving yiz a hard time. Yiz did well tonight. Chin up, Barry. You did good, son.'

Barry smiled at Mick; it was clear that he'd needed to hear that.

'Don't forget we're playing the under-sixteens in a friendly on Saturday. Be here, ten thirty sharp, lads,' said Jimmy.

* * *

The next day in school, Danny was heading to the toilets when he spotted Principal Dunstan on his knees in his office as he walked by.

Danny stopped and looked in.

There were cloths all over the floor, and the Principal looked to be struggling with a burst pipe in his radiator.

Danny knocked on the door then walked into the office.

'Are you alright, Mr Dunstan?' asked Danny.

The Principal looked relieved to see Danny.

'Danny. Good lad. I was moving my desk when I hit the radiator and now it's leaking. There's water everywhere.'

Danny could see that he was holding some cloths around the pipe that was going into the radiator.

'Can I help?' he asked. 'Will I go and get Mr Devlin?'

Mr Devlin was the school caretaker.

'No point,'said Mr Dunstan. 'He's still out on sick leave.'

Principal Dunstan was not handy by any stretch of the imagination. He was much more comfortable standing up making announcements than down on the floor with a box of tools. Danny felt a bit sorry for him.

Danny had an idea.

'I'll get my da,' he said. 'He's at home cos he's after being put on a short week in his job.'

'Do you think he can help?' asked Mr Dunstan, who was starting to get cramp in his legs from kneeling down.

'No problem,' Danny told him. 'He's dead handy with anything like that.'

Danny rushed home and got Mick to come down to the school. Mick wasn't up to much – just reading the job column in the paper, hoping to come across something.

Principal Dunstan was relieved to see Mick walk into his office with a toolbox in his hand.

'Let me have a look at that,' Mick said as he walked over to the radiator, kneeling in front of it. 'Ah! You've just knocked the pipe out. Easily fixed.'

Danny returned back to his class while Mick went to work on the dodgy pipe.

'There you go,' Mick said after a short while. 'All fixed. I don't think that will give you any more problems, but if it does, just get Danny to let me know.'

The principal couldn't thank Mick enough. He persuaded him to join him for a cup of tea in the staff room.

'Danny's been telling me all about your friend's daughter in America.'

'Is that right?' Mick asked. 'Yeah, we even had a fundraiser for her. All Danny's idea, of course. He's a smashing lad.'

'He is,' Mr Dunstan agreed. 'I believe you two are going over there at the end of the month?'

'That's right. Did Danny ask you for the Friday and the Monday off?' asked Mick.

'It's fine.' Mr Dunstan gave him a smile. 'I'm a firm believer in allowing the odd day off from school when it's for such a good cause. Danny was saying that your job is under threat!'

'Yeah! It's only a matter of time before it goes altogether. The good days with work are well and truly over.'

Principal Dunstan could see how worried Mick looked.

'So you have a couple of spare days on your hands now?'

'That's right.' Mick nodded. 'We're on a three-day week at the moment and that could even go down to two by the end of the month.'

'I don't know if you'd be interested in this, but every year around this time, the school has a fundraising day. We do a walk or something along that line. Last year, we had a reading marathon. Anyway, I was wondering if you would be interested in running a kind of football marathon this year for us. Most of the kids on your team are pupils in this school, so you'd be familiar with some of the boys, and of course, the rest would do well to have a proper football coach teach them a few new skills.'

Mick was flattered.

'We usually donate the funds to various different charities. The school would be more than happy to donate any funds raised on the day towards your friend's daughter's operation. What do you think, Mick? Would you be interested?'

'I think that's a wonderful idea,' Mick said. 'And very generous of you.'

'Right, then! I'll get the sponsorship sheets printed up straight away so the boys can get some money in.'

Mick thought that was a great idea, and shook hands with the school principal.

Chapter Thirteen

Under 14s v Under 16s

Mick was in better form for Thursday night's training. Principal Dunstan's supportive words had given him a much-needed lift in confidence.

But that didn't stop Mick from working his players hard and when Saturday's game against Paddy Flynn's under-sixteen's squad came along, friendly or no friendly, Mick prepared his team in the dressing room the very same way he would before any game.

'Come on now lads, settle down,' Jimmy said. 'No more messing now. Come on now, quiet down for Mick.'

Mick waited a few seconds to let the banter settle. 'Okay, lads. I know this is only a friendly today, and most of yiz know one or two of the under-sixteens players.'

Mick glanced over to Paddy Timmons, then to Big Johnner Purcell, who was sitting up the other end of the dressing room, fiddling with his left boot.

'Paddy, Johnner.' Mick flashed them a smile. 'Both your big brothers play for Paddy Flynn's team, isn't that right, lads?'

The two players nodded together.

'Then you guys will know that there's no way that they will want their younger brothers making a show of them,' he went on, 'friendly or no friendly, this game matters. Every game matters.'

'My brother doesn't need me to make a show of him, Mick.' Paddy Timmons laughed. 'He's a big eejit at the best of times.'

All the other players laughed – Jimmy, too.

Mick managed a smile, but he wanted to stay serious.

'I'm telling yiz for your own good, lads.

Paddy Flynn's under-sixteen's are a fine team. They're all big and strong and aren't lacking in the skills department.'

'Yeah, Mick, but they don't have Danny playing for them,' Little John Watson said.

'Go on, Danny!' shouted Doyler. The rest joined in. Mick knew that they had total respect and admiration for their captain. They had all the important things a team needed to show their captain that they were behind him one hundred per cent.

Jimmy let Danny have his moment of glory before he calmed the room again.

'Let's make the most of this game, boys,' said Mick. 'That's all I'm saying. Yiz can be skilful, strong, fast – whatever, but you can't beat experience, and the under-sixteens have two years on yiz. That counts for a lot. Isn't that right, Jimmy?'

'Oh! You're right there, Mick.'

'Jimmy, anything you want to add before we go out?' asked Mick.

'Not really Mick … well, um … just that you know, the runner-up decider is next Saturday and yiz might learn a few things today. That's why we set this game up for yiz. If yiz can compete with these older boys, then maybe yiz might have an edge on Barnfield. That's all really, Mick.'

'Couldn't have said it better, Jimmy,' Mick said.

Mick instructed his team to their feet. It didn't matter if they were playing a friendly. As Mick already said, friendly or no friendly, every game matters, which meant going through the same routine that worked for the team mattered too.

'When you go out onto that pitch, lads, where are you playing?' Mick asked with tremendous pride in his voice. He made sure the under-sixteen's heard every word.

'The Little Croker,' replied his players.

'And how do we play every game?' yelled the manager.

'Like the All Ireland final!' cheered the whole dressing room. Even Heffo, Danny's dog and team mascot, managed a howl of support.

Mick had been true to his word with Barry Sweeney and Doyler. Doyler had been slotted back into his old centre half forward position, while Barry Sweeney wore the number fourteen jersey that had brought him good scores at the beginning of the season.

Billy Stapleton, from Danny and Splinter's class, turned up for the game. Billy loved horses and wasn't particularly known for turning up for football matches, except of course the game earlier in the season against Chapel Hall, when he had stormed across the Little Croker on his horse.

Mick was tying Heffo to the training bag when he noticed Jimmy nodding towards him. Mick twisted his head around to see Billy standing behind him with his hands in his pockets. Billy was blowing a huge bubble from his mouth with his chewing gum.

It burst the second he heard Mick Wilde's voice.

'Not on your horse today?' Mick asked.

Billy almost swallowed his gum.

'Just watching the match,' said Billy.

'I never knew you had any interest in GAA. Haven't seen you at any other game.'

Billy smiled.

'Yeah, but this isn't going to be like any other game. Is it?'

Mick looked at Jimmy.

'What's he on about Jimmy?'

Jimmy shrugged his shoulders.

Billy strolled over to Mick.

'Is that your dog?'

Heffo snarled.

'What do mean this isn't going to be like any other game?' asked Mick.

Billy smiled at Mick – a real cheeky smile, as if to say, *Now! Wouldn't you just love to know!*

The referee blew his whistle, but Paddy Flynn waved his hands at him as if to ask for another few seconds. Somebody – a player – was fixing his boots over at the other line. He was kneeling behind a few of the under sixteen's subs. Nobody could see him.

Then he stood up. All six feet, two inches of him.

'Who the jaysis is that?' cried Jimmy.

Billy laughed.

Everyone on Mick's team, including his subs who, for the first time ever, were delighted not to be starting a game, were dumb struck with fear.

'That's Hammer Hughes.'

'The boxer,' gasped Mick. 'He's only fifteen. What have they been feeding him?'

'National champion boxer,' Jimmy nervously added.

'Do you want to know why he's called the "Hammer"?' Billy asked.

Both Mick and Jimmy turned their head to Billy. 'Why?'

'Cos when he lands his fist on ya, it's like

being hit with a hammer.'

Hammer Hughes, fitness fanatic and boxing champ, was making his debut for both the under-sixteens and the GAA.

'They can't let him play,' Jimmy complained. 'Look at the size of him, and he's a boxer!'

'Champion boxer,' Billy smiled.

'There's nothing we can do, Jimmy. He's not over age and he wants to play GAA, so who are we to stop him?'

Deep down, though, Mick was worried – very worried. He badly wanted this game to build up his team's strength, but now he was worried about Hammer Hughes injuring his players.

Jonathon took a few steps back as the Hammer trotted into the middle of the park and took up his position right adjacent to him.

Jonathon looked terrified.

'I'll jump,' Danny said. Jonathon didn't argue. It was meant to be his turn to jump. He gladly changed positions with Danny.

Danny looked up and faced the gruesome stare of the Hammer.

Jonathon feared for Danny. He knew how brave his cousin was, but this was crazy. This over sized Hammer lad looked like he was ready to kill someone, and there was just one person between him and the ball – Danny.

'Ready boys!?' the referee asked, then he looked at Hammer again, as if making sure that he was a boy.

Danny nodded to the referee, who had given him a look and a little smile as if to say, *Rather you than me!*

The whistle blew and the ball was thrown in.

Mick put his face in his hands. Jimmy had just finished chewing all of the nails on his left hand and was now halfway through his right hand. Heffo barked, and Larry ran up to the line with the same expression on his face that everyone else had the second they saw the Hammer.

But everyone did the exact same thing the

second they saw Danny pull off one of the craftiest manoeuvres they had ever seen.

They all cheered! Even the subs on Paddy Flynn's side of the pitch.

Danny had managed to do what none of his teammates were able to do with their fear. He acknowledged that even though Hammer Hughes was built like King Kong, it was still his first time ever on a football pitch, and Danny remembered Mick telling everyone how much experience meant.

Hammer Hughes was so big that he hardly needed to jump at all for the ball. The second he caught it, Danny punched it down, knocking it out of the Hammer's hands. The ball bounced and before the Hammer had a chance to steal it back, Danny fisted it up and over the Hammer's head and caught it, then spun around the under sixteen's number nine and rocketed a low pass out to Paul Kiely, Crokes' right half forward.

Danny and the Hammer had looked like

David and Goliath as they waited for the referee to throw the ball in, but Danny Wilde had
overpowered the beast with skill and quick
thinking and left the Hammer looking small
and humiliated in the centre of the pitch.

Paul Kiely was beaten to Danny's pass by the
under sixteen's left half back, who scooped up
the ball with ease then swiftly turned Kiely
inside out with a left shimmy, followed by a
right.

The left halfback then unleashed a long and
high ball up towards his centre half forward.

Alan Whelan put in a good firm challenge for
the ball, but lost out to the number eleven, who
quickly shifted the ball out to his right full
forward.

The under-sixteen's right full forward went
on a powerful solo, beating both his marker,
Kevin Kinsella, the Crokes' left full back, and
big Johnner Purcell, the Crokes full back.

Then with one final glance at the Crokes'
goal, he struck the ball with accuracy into the

top left corner of the goal.

Crokes were already a goal down, even after Danny's masterful manoeuvres in the middle of the field.

'Come on, Crokes,' Danny groaned as he clapped his hands together, and made eye contact with each and every one of his players.

Hammer Hughes had just been given a crash course in GAA, the previous Tuesday and Thursday's training and was still struggling to grasp how to actually get himself into the game.

So Hammer did the next best thing. He stuck to his man like super glue. That meant that everywhere Danny went, the Hammer followed.

Danny was fast – very fast – and much more agile than the Hammer, but the under sixteen's debut rookie was a fighter – literally – and that meant never giving up until the bell rang or in their case, the half time whistle blew.

Eventually, to Danny and all his team mate's relief, the referee did blow the half time whistle, and Mick Wilde's team slumped over to their coach, tired and bruised and behind by a score of 0-0 to 1-3.

Mick gave his players a couple of minutes to catch their breath before he delivered his half-time talk.

Larry felt the urge to have a word or two with his brother.

Jimmy dropped what he was doing and joined them. Jimmy always felt that Larry was trying to move in on his turf. Jimmy was assistant coach, and if anything was to be discussed at half-time, Jimmy Murphy wanted to be in on it.

'They're having a hard time out there, Mick,' Larry said. 'Those lads are far stronger than them. Do you not think this will only damage their confidence for next week's game?'

'No!' huffed Jimmy.

Mick smiled at Jimmy. He appreciated how much Larry got on Jimmy's nerves, but he also valued his brother's opinion. After all, Larry was a fine GAA player in his youth, and knew a thing or two about the sport.

'I get what you're saying, Larry. I've seen Paddy Flynn's team in action a few times and always felt that our boys could give them a good run, but it's only when you actually put an under fourteen's in a game against an under sixteen's that you really see the difference two years makes.'

Jimmy felt the desire to speak again. 'I think our lads are doing great.'

'They're doing superb,' Larry agreed. 'I just think that their heads might drop if they get slaughtered.'

'That's not going to happen,' Mick said. 'They're fighters. Let's see how they get on in the second half.'

Mick turned around to address his team.

'Okay boys! How are yiz after that grilling?'

He didn't get much of a response – just a groan or two.

Maybe Larry's right! thought Mick. *I'll have to try and lift them. I'll get Danny to have a word or two.*

Mick looked over to Danny, who was the only player on the team who didn't seem phased at all by the beating they were getting from their older club players.

'What do you think, Danny?' asked Mick. 'Can we give these fellas a game in the second half?'

'I don't see why not,' Danny answered, sounding like a natural-born leader.

Danny stood up.

'Look, lads. We were all freaked out when we saw Hammer Hughes jogging onto the pitch, but take away his size and his pretty face and there's not much left to worry about.'

All the players laughed.

'Yiz have to forget about them being bigger and older than yiz, and start playing football. Anyone of yiz can go in for a ball and win it, and anyone of yiz can score a point or even a goal. Just do what we do every week, and start believing in yourselves–'

Danny's words of encouragement were

interrupted by the referee's whistle.

'Go on now, boys,' Larry cheered. Danny's speech had even convinced Larry that the game wasn't a waste of time.

'Yeah! Go on, lads,' Jimmy added. 'Get stuck in to them!'

Mick said nothing. He was so proud of Danny. *I better watch my job!* thought Mick. *Danny showed real coaching potential there!*

Even though the Hammer Hughes didn't impress Paddy Flynn with his inexperienced flapping around in the first half, Paddy felt that it would be better to leave the rookie on for the second half, if only to learn a thing or two from Danny.

Darren Lyons, the under sixteen's number nine, nominated himself to jump against Danny for the throw in. Darren was determined to show the Hammer how not to be made a fool of by a younger club player.

Danny asked Jonathon if he wanted to jump; once Danny had one hundred per cent convinced Jonathon that he wouldn't have to face the Hammer, Jonathon accepted.

The whistle was blown and the second half was away.

Darren Lyons easily beat Jonathon to the ball, but Jonathon put a fair challenge to him and the ball fell lose into the path of Danny and the Hammer.

The Hammer had been watching Danny carefully in the first half and had learnt a thing or two about this new sport he had chosen to play.

The Hammer craftily turned his back to Danny and shielded the ball from the Crokes' captain.

Danny, who never pulled out of a challenge and gave everything to win every ball, crashed into the Hammer's back side and was sent tumbling head first across the middle of the field.

'Is he alright?' gasped Jimmy.

Mick watched, worried, as Danny slowly picked himself up. He was a bit shaken, but not injured.

'Watch this, Jimmy.' Mick smiled with relief.

Danny shook himself off as he got to his feet, and nodded over toward the Hammer with a smile.

The Hammer had sent a good solid pass up field to his forward line, and then turned around to see if Danny was okay. Danny knew that Hammer Hughes wasn't like Sean 'Dirty' Dempsey or Deco Savage. He had respect for his opponent no matter what the sport.

Danny gave the Hammer a thumbs up, then sprinted to help his defence keep the under sixteen's from scoring yet again.

Big Johnner Purcell was the first to show that he had taken on board every word that Danny had said when he threw himself, hands first, at a thundering shot from the under sixteen's centre full forward to reflect the ball away from goal and into the path of Darren Ward, Crokes' right halfback.

The Crokes' number five heard Danny calling for the ball. Danny had found a free space between two of the under sixteen's players. Darren Ward lobbed a lovely pass over the under sixteen's number twelve, straight into Danny's hands.

Danny turned sharply and went on a Danny solo.

Hammer Hughes lunged himself towards Danny, trying to knock Danny and the ball to the ground, but Danny clipped the ball over the Hammer's head, and like lightning, he side-stepped to his left, leaving the Hammer to fall face first and skid along the grass.

The Hammer rolled over and sat bolt up. He looked like a soldier camouflaged from head to toe in mud.

Billy Stapleton laughed so loud that he could be heard from both ends of the pitch, but he swiftly shut up and turned his head away and began whistling as soon as he realised that the Hammer was staring over at him.

As Danny powered towards the goal, he seemed to pick up momentum.

'Over here Danny!' Doyler called. He had left his player and moved into the space between Splinter and Barry Sweeney.

Danny lobbed a perfect pass over Doyler's marker, the under sixteen's centre halfback.

Doyler caught the ball, then took one quick look at goal and had a shot.

Doyler's shot fell short, and Barry Sweeney charged in to win the ball against the under sixteen's goalkeeper and full back. The goalkeeper bravely lunged himself at the ball, punching it away from goal.

The ball flew through the air towards Danny. Danny caught the ball and like Doyler, took one quick glance at goal.

Danny released the ball and hooked it around the chaos in front of the goalmouth, smashing it into the top right corner of the net.

'GOAL!' Jimmy screamed as he and Larry both danced around Mick.

Heffo saw all the excitement and wanted to join in so he spun around the training bag, barking like mad until eventually, there was no more lead. The team mascot decided that it would be more fun to resume chewing on the straps of the bag, and occasionally stopping to snarl at Billy.

Paddy Flynn clapped his hands in admiration and looked over towards Mick.

Mick put his hands in the air. He had a huge smile on his face. Paddy gave Mick the thumbs up. Although their teams were competing against each other, they were from the same club, and Paddy was pleased that Mick's team would go away with some pride and experience from this friendly, to help them in their final game against local arch-rivals, Barnfield.

Danny's goal had lifted his side's confidence, and straight from the kick out, Doyler won the ball and sent it over for a point.

That was the last score from Mick's team, and the under sixteen's picked themselves back up and went on to score another goal and two points, ending the game, 2-5 to 1-1.

Mick rallied around all his players, congratulating them for all their brave efforts.

Paddy Flynn made all of his players shake hands with Mick's players, and then he gave the Crokes' under fourteens a few words of praise and encouragement.

Mick had got it right. It was indeed a priceless game to help prepare them for the up coming showdown with Barnfield.

Danny made it his business to particularly give a few words of encouragement to the Hammer Hughes as both teams trotted back together to the dressing rooms.

Danny patted the Hammer on the back. 'Good game.'

The Hammer pushed Danny and laughed, but he was just fooling about.

'You're a savage player.' The Hammer gave him a smile. 'Thanks for the work out. Ya ran rings around me.'

'Thanks. Anytime!'

Both players laughed.

'Are you going to stick with it?' asked Danny as he approached his dressing room.

'Yeah, I am,' the Hammer said. 'You'll have to come down to the boxing club some time, and I'll teach you a few moves.'

'Are ya mad?' Danny laughed. 'And ruin this pretty face?'

Danny and the Hammer chatted for a few minutes and then the Hammer disappeared into his dressing room. Danny could still hear him laughing after the door was closed.

Who would have ever thought that Danny would tame the beast that everyone feared?

Give Danny Wilde a football and put him on a pitch, and he could do just about anything.

Chapter Fourteen

A Football Email

Later that night, Danny was e-mailing Clara when Mick came into the room with Danny's phone.

'Your phone is making a buzzing noise, Danny. I think it's a text message.'

'Thanks, Da,' Danny said as he took his phone from Mick.

He glanced at the message.

'It's from Trinity.'

'Oh, yeah?' Mick smiled. 'All's going well, I see.'

'She wants to know if I want to go to a film on Tuesday night. We'll be training so I'll see if she can make it another night instead. Is that alright, Da?'

Mick nodded.

'No problem. Actually, Tuesday night will be fine. We won't have any training. There'll be enough practice at the football marathon in your school that day. But it *is* a school night so make sure you go to an early film, so you're not out too late.'

'Nice one, Da. Her mam will drop and collect us.'

Mick noticed that Danny was spending a lot of time on the computer; he had never shown much interest in the computer, except every now and then to do a project for school.

'Is that school work?' Mick asked.

'Eh! No,' Danny replied. 'I'm just e-mailing Clara. You know like, about the match and that. She likes to hear that kind of stuff, Da.'

Mick's smile stretched from ear to ear.

'Really? Is that so, son? Do you have two girl-friends on the go?'

Danny pushed Mick away.

'Snap out of it. Clara's just a mate. A football mate.' He laughed.

Mick left Danny in peace to continue his e-mail to Clara.

Danny wrote:

Alright, Clara!

I had a match today. Just letting you know how we did, cos I know you like hearing about GAA and stuff. We played a friendly against the under sixteen's. They were brill! It was a savage match. They were much stronger than us, but we got stuck into them.

They had a new player. Hammer Hughes is his name. He's a boxer, a deadly boxer and it was his first GAA match ever. He was huge. I was planking it cos he was in midfield against me, but it went okay. I'm still in one piece. He's actually a nice bloke. He came over to me after the game and said that I was a good player. He said that it was like playing against a tiger, the way I prowled around the pitch, hunting the ball down then moving in for a lethal strike.

I thought that was a mad thing to say, but it was nice to get a compliment like that.

My da says a big hello to everyone and he's looking

forward to coming over to see yiz all at the end of the month.

We got the tickets. They were a good price, which was good cos my da's job is looking bad at the moment. He thinks that he's going to lose it all together. Things are like that over here at the moment. Everybody is losing their jobs. I hope my da doesn't lose his job cos he really needs it. I know he gets lonely sometimes without my mam and his job and the GAA keep him going.

Anyway, enough misery. Here's some good news. We're doing a sponsored football marathon in our school on Tuesday, and guess what? It's for you. My da was in the school fixing a broken pipe for the principal. Dunstan – that's the principal. He's mad! But I'll tell you about him another time. Anyway, he thought it was great that the Crokes were doing the fundraiser for you, so he asked my da if he'd like to run the sponsored marathon for you, as well.

My da thought that was a deadly idea, so it's going ahead on Tuesday. I'll let you know how we get on. It should be animal!

That's all I can think about. Oh, yeah, we're playing Barnfield next Saturday at home. It looks like it's for the runner up spot in the league, so it's a big one.

Wish us luck!

Talk soon.

Danny.

Just as Danny had finished the last line, Mick came back into the room.

'I meant to tell you, Danny, I've got an interview on Tuesday at four thirty.'

Danny spun around on his chair.

'Where?'

'Mullins' Builder Providers.'

'Will you make it, Da?' Danny was worried. 'What about the sponsored marathon?'

'I'll be grand, Danny. If I have to leave a bit early, it'll be okay. I'll pop home and have a quick shower. Mullins' isn't that far away. By the way, how's your sponsor card coming on. Is it full yet?'

'Nearly, Da. There are only a few lines left.

Granny's coming around on Tuesday evening so I'll get her to sponsor me before I go to the pictures with Trinity.'

Danny was worried about his father and the whole situation with his work. Mick had been in the same job for a good few years and there was never a problem with money. But Danny knew it wasn't just about money where Mick was concerned. Just having a job meant a lot to Mick.

'Do you think you'll get the job?' Danny asked.

Mick shrugged.

'I'm not sure, son. Jimmy knows them down there and he recommended me, so fingers crossed.'

Danny turned back around and clicked to send his e-mail to Clara.

I hope Da gets that job! thought Danny.

Chapter Fifteen

The Marathon Begins

Mick and Danny left early for school on Tuesday morning. Jimmy was there, too. He had taken the day off to help Mick run the sponsored marathon.

Everybody turned up with their sports bags, and the atmosphere was buzzing if only because the marathon meant a whole day off from the usual boring school routine.

Mick followed Principal Dunstan into the staff room where he was introduced to all the teachers.

'This is Mick Wilde,' Mr Dunstan introduced him. 'He's going to be giving you all your instructions for the day.'

Mick was a bit embarrassed. The last time he

was in front of so many teachers was when he was a young boy.

'How ya, everybody?'

He smiled, then looked back toward Principal Dunstan for some guidance.

'We have all the boys in the main hall,' Mr Dunstan went on. 'What we're going to do is separate them all into groups. The first and second years together – third years on their own and fifth and sixth years together.'

Principal Dunstan then looked at Mick.

'Would you like to take it from there, Mick?'

Mick nodded.

'Um, well, what we were thinking of doing was running mini leagues throughout the day. Like, for example, the first and second years will be one league and so on. I think that's a fair way of doing it. That way we can keep the age levels close together.'

Everyone agreed. Some even managed to pull their lips away from their cups of tea to murmur in agreement.

'Tell them the fun bit Mick,' Mr Dunstan said.

'Oh yeah!' Mick chuckled nervously. 'Um, well, I won't be able to manage all of this on my own of course. I have a friend with me. Jimmy Murphy. He's assistant coach of my own team, the Crokes. You might know his son Damien.'

There were a couple of eyebrows raised. Damien Murphy – AKA Splinter – had an unforgettable presence in the school.

Mick continued.

'Anyway, we'll need some help so that's where you guys come in.'

Mr Breen put his hand up to ask Mick a question. Mick thought that was hilarious – a schoolteacher with his hand up.

'I presume the boys have brought in their own gear. How will we distinguish them if we don't have sets of jerseys?'

'Thought of that one,' Mick said. 'We managed to gather a load of bibs – yellow, orange, red and blue ones. We'll use them as jerseys.'

Mr Breen was impressed, as were the rest of the teachers.

Mick thanked everyone for their help and, in particular, he thanked Principal Dunstan, for suggesting the idea of the sponsored marathon to help Clara.

There were two GAA pitches in Danny's school, which was a good thing as there were a lot of matches to get through.

Because there were so many classes to compete, it was agreed that the four third year classes would compete in a soccer league, over on the one and only soccer pitch at the far end of the school grounds, under the supervision of Mr Hooper.

That left year one and two, which together consisted of eight classes, to compete on the first GAA pitch, and year five and six, which, also consisted of eight classes to compete on the second GAA pitch.

* * *

It took Mick and Jimmy a whole hour to organise

everyone, and get the matches going.

The first games started at ten. Each match lasted thirty minutes – fifteen minutes each way with a quick turn around between halves.

As there were eight teams in each league, Mick decided that it would be a knockout league, so that there would be four teams left after the first round of games. That meant that the four successful teams would go on to play in a semi-final after lunch, and then the final, which would be held around a quarter to three.

Mick had made up his mind that he wouldn't be involved in Danny's league. He thought that would be best for Danny. Danny's teammates on the Crokes were used to the father and son thing, but Danny's fellow school pupils weren't.

The morning passed quickly without any problems. All the teachers fitted with ease into whatever role Mick and Jimmy gave to them. Of course not every pupil and teacher was familiar with all the rules, but that didn't matter.

It was a great day and everyone was pulling together for one cause – Clara.

Chapter Sixteen

'We Didn't Lose'

After lunch, everyone gathered on the first pitch. There was great excitement now, as all the teams who were knocked out in the first round became supporters, so there were good crowds at each of the two GAA pitches, and to add to this, the third year's soccer marathon was over so they joined in the support.

Mick and Jimmy were referees for the two fifth and sixth year league semi finals, and Mr Breen and Mr Gray were nominated by the other teachers to referee the first and second year semi finals.

Danny's team had made it to the semis. There were three other players from Danny's club in his class. Splinter, Doyler and Liam

Darcy, the Crokes' goalkeeper, which really helped them progress into the semis.

Danny's class was drawn against Sean 'Dirty' Dempsey's class for the first semi.

Mick and Jimmy knew it and were both eager to see the match, but they had their own games to referee.

Mr Davis was in charge of Danny's team and he had followed Mick's instructions all morning as how to manage the team fairly. Because there were thirty boys in each class, it was only fair to give everyone a few minutes play in each game, so Mr Davis had to keep swapping things around. In one game earlier that morning, he put one set of fifteen players out in the first half and then changed the team entirely by playing the other fifteen boys in the second half.

Danny was disappointed to be left on the line for the start of his semi final.

Dempsey didn't waste any time in teasing Danny as he waited in the middle of the pitch for Mr Gray to throw the ball in.

* * *

All watches ticked two o'clock and on Mick's earlier instructions, all whistles were blown together and all footballs were thrown in.

Danny watched enviously as Dempsey overpowered his opponent with ease to win the throw in for his class and stampede through not one, but three of Danny's class mates.

I wish I were out there! thought Danny. *I'd stop him in his tracks. The state of him, showing off in front of everyone. He's only able to do that because Mr Davis put the weaker side out first.*

Danny was right! Mr Davis had put the weaker side out first and that really made Dempsey look good as he scored three consecutive points in the first half, along with setting up a goal for his full forward after he caught Liam Darcy's fluffed kick out, just after Dempsey had scored his third point.

It was half-time, and Danny's class was behind by 1-3 to 0-1. The half-time turn arounds were quick, so Danny knew that if he had a chance of being played in the second half, then he better get himself right under the nose of Mr Davis.

The schoolteacher glanced over the waving hands of all the boys who desperately wanted to be picked. Danny had hoped that he would just do a complete swap around like earlier that morning and he didn't even care if that meant good players, such as Splinter and Liam Darcy, not playing in the second half.

Danny had one player on his mind – Dempsey.

Finally, Danny was picked, but to his disappointment, Dempsey wasn't playing in the second half.

Dempsey knew that he was only going to play in the first half and that was why he put on an outstanding display of talent. The Barnfield midfielder took full advantage of the middle of the field not having the super talented Danny Wilde on it.

Danny almost burst a gut trying to get his class back in with a chance of progressing to the school marathon final, but it just wasn't enough and there just wasn't the time to do it. Danny had scored two brilliant points, but both Splinter and Doyler, his club forwards had been replaced with five minutes to go and that really depleted his chances of setting one of them up for a goal.

The match finished, 1- 5 to 0-4 in favour of Dempsey's class.

Danny was devastated!

Both Jimmy and Mick raced over to Danny's pitch to get the result of the game; when they saw Dempsey leaping in the air and making gestures at them, they knew that their son's class had been knocked out.

Danny and Splinter slowly walked over to their fathers.

Danny put his hands in the air. He had a face

the length of the football pitch he'd just played on.

Splinter fussed.

'It's not *fair*. That Davis eejit left Danny on the line for the whole of the first half.'

'Be quiet!' Jimmy said. 'Don't talk about your teacher like that.'

'He's not my teacher.'

Jimmy scoured Splinter with a look that made sure his son's lips wouldn't open again for a while.

Mick patted Danny on the back.

'Well done, son.'

'But we lost, Da,' said Danny.

'We didn't lose, Danny. Today was great and look what we've achieved. We've raised tons of money for Clara. That's all that matter.'

'That's right, Danny,' Jimmy added. 'Don't worry about that Dempsey fella. We'll wipe the smile off his face on Saturday.'

Danny looked over towards Dempsey who was still celebrating.

You can say that again, Jimmy! he thought.

* * *

Mick had to rush off to get ready for his interview. He thanked Principal Dunstan again for all the school's support, and then he left Jimmy to take charge of the fifth and sixth year final.

Danny waved to his dad and wished him good luck, then sat down to watch the older final, as he didn't want to see the final that he should have been playing in.

He'd seen enough of Sean Dempsey for one day.

It was the second half of the fifth and sixth year final. It was a good game and Danny and Splinter were enjoying the action when they heard a commotion coming from the first and second year final on the other pitch.

'Come on,' said Splinter.

Danny and Splinter ran over to see what all the fuss was.

Sean Dempsey's class was losing to another

second year class by two points and there was just a couple of minutes left on the clock.

Dempsey had fouled one of the other team's players and got himself into a tussle with him earlier in the game. The other player hadn't forgot Dempsey's dirty tackle and decided to get his own back when Dirty Dempsey taunted him behind the referee's back.

The other player snapped and a fight broke out.

Both Dempsey and the other player were sent off, but Dempsey had caused enough fuss to upset the game and the schoolteacher who was referee.

The teacher almost immediately blew the full time whistle.

Dempsey's class had won their final.

Chapter Seventeen

A Date With Trinity

Principal Dunstan had bought small trophies for each of the winning classes, along with medals for each class that had collected the most money with their sponsor cards.

Danny and Splinter had to stay behind after the presentation to help Jimmy and one or two of the teachers to gather all of Mick's gear and footballs.

Mick wasn't home when Danny got back from school, but Danny's Granny, Maureen, was waiting at the door.

'There you are, Danny pet.' Granny Maureen smiled. 'Where's your daddy? There's no answer.'

Danny was exhausted. 'He's at a job interview.'

'Oh! God bless him. That's right, pet. I hope he gets it. He sounded terrible worried on the phone last night.'

Danny had had a shower and was making his Granny a cup of tea when Mick finally arrived home.

'Did you get the job?' asked Granny Maureen. Mick had hardly closed the door behind him.

Mick's head dropped and he shrugged.

'Don't worry, son. There'll be other jobs.'

Danny rushed in from the kitchen, but he knew the second he saw Mick's face that it was bad news.

Mick threw his coat on the armchair, but it slid off and fell onto the floor. Mick wasn't even bothered to pick it up. Danny picked his father's coat up and hung it up under the stairs

'Do you want a cup of tea, Da?' Danny asked.

He didn't know how to react to his father's disappointment. That job business was very confusing to Danny. It wasn't like his football. Danny knew how to cope with disappointments with football and his da was usually the one who would say that everything would be okay, but not this time. This was a type of worrying that Danny hadn't seen in his father since his mam died.

Even when Mick had his stroke last year, things didn't seem so bad.

'Thanks, son,' said Mick.

'Don't worry, Da. Things will pick up. Maybe your own job will get busy again,' Danny tried hard to lift his father's spirits.

'I don't know, Danny. I think it's only a matter of time before it's gone altogether.'

'What happened at the interview?'

'Flamin' waste of time,' Mick said. 'There wasn't a job after all.'

'But I thought Jimmy had put a good word in for you,' said Danny.

'He did. But there wasn't a job going. The boss and Jimmy must have got their wires crossed. I think he must have just told Jimmy to ask me to come in for an interview just to shut

Jimmy up. Apparently, Jimmy was raving on about me.'

'Ah! Well, at least Jimmy tried, Da.'

'I know, son,' Mick said. 'Jimmy's a good mate. I just got my hopes up, though, and now I'm back to square one again. That's all. I'll get over it.'

Mick sipped his tea in the kitchen while Granny Maureen filled out Danny's sponsor card.

'There, pet! Two euro.'

'Thanks, Gran.' Danny gave her a grateful smile.

Granny Maureen put her hand on Danny's arm as he took the sponsor card from her.

'Don't worry about your daddy,' she said. 'He's solid as a rock. He'll get yiz through these tough times – job or no job. You can be sure of that.'

Danny just nodded.

Granny Maureen stood up and put her coat on.

'I'm off now, Michael,' she called out to the

kitchen. 'I have to go and visit Vera Burke.'

'See you, Mam,' Mick called back with a more upbeat lilt to his voice.

Danny didn't want to bombard his dad with questions about the interview, so he left him to himself for a while and turned on the computer to see if there was an e-mail from Clara.

There was, which cheered up Danny. He loved the new friendship that he had found.

Hi Tiger Boots!

I hope you don't mind me giving you this nickname? I think it really suits you. You're just the best—

Just then, the doorbell rang.

'I'll get it,' shouted Mick, who was upstairs.

Danny could hear voices from the hall. Then, he clearly heard,

'Are you sure your mammy won't come in?'

Suddenly, Danny jumped up.

TRINITY!

He'd forgotten all about their date!

Danny jumped up and ran out to the kitchen.

'Go on in to him,' Mick said to Trinity. 'He's just on the computer. Another e-mail from Clara, no doubt.'

Mick closed the door behind him and went out to say hello to Trinity's mother.

Danny came in from the kitchen to find Trinity standing in the sitting room.

'How ya, Trinity?' Danny smiled at her. 'I was waiting for you to call around.'

Trinity smiled, but a worried look lingered on her face.

Danny asked Trinity to sit down while he ran up to get his jacket. She sat down on the couch opposite the computer.

Danny was a couple of minutes upstairs. He couldn't find his hair gel! He wanted to look his best for Trinity. A soon as he was happy with his hair, he grabbed some money from his top drawer and threw his jacket on.

Trinity was sitting at the edge of the couch when Danny popped his head around the door of the sitting room.

He was all smiles as he walked toward her.

'Are we off?'

Trinity smiled back. 'We sure are!'

* * *

Danny could hardly get more than two words out of Trinity all night, and when they were heading back to the meeting point that they had arranged with Trinity's mam after the film was over, Danny decided to confront Trinity.

'Did you not like the film?'

Trinity just shrugged.

'Did I do something wrong?' was Danny's second question.

Trinity shook her head and looked at Danny.

'I don't know. Did you?'

Danny was confused. *What's the matter with her?* he thought.

Danny got the silent treatment in the car on the way home, too, and when he said goodbye to Trinity and asked her if she was coming to see his last game of the season against Barnfield, Trinity could only commit to a 'maybe'. That's if there was nothing else to do that day.

Mick was watching a film when Danny walked into the sitting room.

'How was the flicks, son. Good film?' Mick asked, clearly in a better mood than he was when Danny left.

Danny just looked at Mick, and turned around.

'I'm going to bed, Da,' he said and closed the door behind him.

First, my da is in the horrors over his job and now he's in great form and Trinity is in the horrors! I can't wait for Boston. I need a break from this place! Danny thought before he fell asleep that night.

Chapter Eighteen

Bad Behaviour

It was Saturday, 21 November, the day of the last league game in the under fourteen's division 1.

The Crokes had had a very poor start to the season, but they gained great confidence with their powerful run in the Féile during the summer.

They were going into the game on the back of a straight five-match winning streak, beating Terrystown both home and away, Rockmount away, Darnville at home and Fergally away.

To add to this super run, the Crokes were the only team in the season to take a point off Chapel Hall when they drew with them away.

Chapel Hall had already been announced as league victors and the game between the

Crokes and Barnfield would decide the runner up. Terrystown had been in the running, too, but they slipped out of contention in the previous game when they were beaten by Chapel Hall at home.

* * *

Mick had put all his job worries to one side to concentrate on the crucial game. Danny had woken up with the same attitude, and even though he had heard nothing from Trinity all week and was concerned about their relationship, just like his father, Danny switched into GAA mode to prepare himself for the match.

Danny was helping Mick carry out the team gear when Splinter came across the road.

'All set captain,' Splinter said and he stood to attention and saluted Danny.

Danny laughed.

'You're stone mad, Splinter.'

Jimmy closed the hall door behind him. His whole family was waiting in the garden.

In fact, neighbours spilled out from their

houses. They zipped up coats. Put on hats and tied scarves. Littlestown Crokes were never short of support when it came to a big game, but whenever they played local adversaries Barnfield, it always sparked extra attention.

Mick took a look down the road, watching everyone head in the same direction – toward the playing fields, then he gave Jimmy a thumbs-up and the two coaches grabbed a bag each.

The match was scheduled for an early start at 11 am and Mick had arranged with all his players to meet at the dressing rooms at ten thirty.

The dressing rooms had been opened at a quarter past ten so when Mick, Jimmy, Danny and Splinter arrived, the rest of Mick's team was already inside.

As Danny and Splinter were heading into the dressing rooms, they heard someone imitating the sound of a chicken.

Danny knew exactly who it was before he even spun around. Standing across the yard, outside the away team's dressing room was Deco Savage. Deco was flapping his arms and making the chicken noise towards Danny.

Splinter grabbed Danny's arm.

'Leave it alone, Danny,' advised Splinter. 'He's only a muppet!'

Then, to add to Danny's humiliation, Sean and Tommy Dempsey, walked through the gates.

Dempsey burst out laughing and joined in the slagging.

'Are ya getting your game today, Wilde?' He teased. 'Of course you are. Sure, don't you play for your daddy's team?'

That was the straw that broke the camels back as far as Danny was concerned. He had never been in a situation before where a player suggested that he only got his game because of his dad being coach. Everyone on Danny's team knew that he was the best player on the team and that he worked harder than anyone to earn his place.

Danny snapped, 'Is that right, Dempsey? I heard your da tried his hand at coaching himself. Didn't do a great job against Darnville last week, did he?'

That wiped the smirk off Tommy Dempsey's face.

As things were heating up outside and the noise carried on into the dressing rooms, both Mick and the Barnfield manager came out of their rooms to see what was going on.

Mick wasn't surprised when he saw Danny and Dempsey face to face in the middle of the yard. Mick marched over to Danny and grabbed his arm.

'Inside, now!'

The Barnfield manager did the same to Sean.

Tommy Dempsey's smirk returned to his face, but only for the benefit of Mick Wilde.

Mick could hear Tommy titter as he marched Danny back over to the home dressing room. Mick turned around and scoured Tommy.

He didn't say anything and he didn't have to.

He nodded to the Barnfield manager and received a nod back. Both coaches had equal respect for each other and both knew how much of a waster Tommy Dempsey was for allowing the two boys to wind each other up to the point of almost scrapping.

Danny sat down between little John Watson and Alan Whelan. He knew that Mick was furious with him so he kept his head down and just got on with getting changed for the game.

Mick was very quiet while the boys were getting themselves ready; there was a real possibility that he would put Danny on the line for his bad behaviour out in the yard.

Mick looked to Jimmy and gave him the nod.

'Right, lads! Everyone listen up,' Jimmy announced, and then he blew lightly on his whistle.

Danny's heart beat rapid as he waited for his dad to speak. Danny knew more than anyone that Mick Wilde took his coaching more seriously than anyone else in the sport, and he knew that he might just have put his dad in an awkward position.

'Right, lads!' Mick spoke finally. That was something. 'First of all, I just want to say a few words about a certain incident outside a few minutes ago.'

Here it comes! thought Danny.

Mick looked over towards Danny.

'Under no circumstances do Jimmy or I condone any kind of fighting on or off the field. I know things can get a bit heated during a match, and that's understandable, but there's no excuse for getting into a scrap with another player before a game.'

Normally, Jimmy would jump in and make it heard that he was in total agreement with Mick; he kept quiet this time.

Danny bit on his lip. *If I keep my mouth shut, maybe Da will leave it at that!*

Unfortunately, Splinter couldn't keep his mouth shut.

'It wasn't Danny's fault, Mick.'

'Damien!' Jimmy chided, looking over to his son.

'It wasn't, Da,' Splinter protested. 'Deco Savage was winding Danny up, calling him a chicken 'cos Danny wouldn't show off in front of Trinity at the fair, and then Dempsey started slagging Danny over losing in the football marathon in school.'

Mick looked at Jimmy, then at Splinter, and finally fixed his eyes upon Danny, who was waiting for sentence.

'Fair enough, Damien,' said Mick. 'But, you don't play into their hands and get yourself into a fight. Danny, don't you see that that's exactly what they wanted from you? They probably planned it to get you into trouble before the game even started.'

Mick looked at Jimmy.

'I think you could be right there, Mick,' Jimmy said. 'We don't want to give them what they're looking for, do we?'

Danny perked up.

Mick returned his eyes to Danny.

'If that ever happens again, you're dropped. Do you understand, Danny?'

Danny nodded, and then winked a *Thanks, buddy!* over at Splinter when he noticed Mick talking to Jimmy.

There was a knock on the door from the referee.

'Right, boys,' Mick said. He glanced all around the dressing room, executing the same pre-match routine, by making eye contact with each and every one of his players. 'Who'd had thought boys that we would be back here on the Little Croker playing Barnfield in the last game of the season again.'

'But we're not playing for the league title,' Doyler interrupted.

'That doesn't matter,' Mick responded. 'We have a chance to clinch the runner up spot and against Barnfield. There's nothing wrong with second best, isn't that right Jimmy?'

'Spot on, Mick,' Jimmy said with a nod.

'Yiz have put in a superb second half to the

season lads, and myself and Jimmy are dead proud of yiz, no matter the result of this game. But guess what, boys?' Mick smiled at his team. 'This could be the best game of your lives if you want it to be. Enjoy your football and you'll always be a winner!' Mick yelled. 'Now, all on your feet.'

An army of lads stomped the dressing room floor.

'When you go out onto that pitch, lads, where are you playing?' asked Mick.

'On the Little Croker!' came the reply.

'And how do we play every game?'

'Like the all Ireland final!'

Chapter Nineteen

Tiger Boots

Mick had given Danny a second chance. Of course, Danny was team captain and the Crokes' best player, but that didn't make him invincible.

It was agreed that Jonathon would jump for the throw in as Dempsey had stepped forward.

Danny could see both Dempsey and Savage trying to make eye contact with him to further wind him up, but Danny wasn't having any of it. He wanted to show everyone that he was better than that – better than them, not just at football, but also in the way he carried himself and represented his team as captain.

Danny had one last look over to the line just to give Mick a thumbs-up when he noticed Trinity and Lowry walking up towards Larry who was standing near Jimmy.

Regina was trailing behind with Granny Maureen. Now, all the Wilde family was here and, most importantly to Danny, Trinity had decided to come after all.

That gave Danny a real boost.

'All set, lads?' asked the referee.

Jonathon and Danny nodded. Dempsey and Savage nodded.

'Best of luck, boys. I know this is a big game, but keep it clean.'

The whistle was blown and the ball was in the air.

Dempsey out-jumped Jonathon and fisted the ball down to Savage. Danny pounced toward Savage like the tiger that Hammer Hughes had compared him to, but Savage cleverly side-stepped Danny's approach and left the Crokes' captain face down on the turf.

Jonathon could hear Dempsey laughing at Danny, so he stuck a sneaky elbow into Dempsey's side as he ran past him. Dempsey tried to retaliate, but Danny quickly jumped to his feet and pulled Jonathon away.

Savage had kicked the ball out to his left half forward who beat Darren Ward, the Crokes' right half back, then sent a low pass back across the Crokes' defence to his centre half forward.

The Crokes number six, Alan Whelan, jumped onto the back of the Barnfield forward and sent him crashing to the ground.

The referee blew his whistle. Barnfield had a free kick.

Sean Dempsey was one of the best kickers for Barnfield, and that was one of the reasons why he had made it onto the Dublin development squad.

Dempsey took the ball to hand, took a few steps forward, then kicked a massive high shot toward the Crokes' goal. The ball seemed to stay in the air forever, but as it came down, it was noticeable from where Mick and Jimmy were standing that it was going to fall short.

'Defend!' Jimmy roared.

Liam Darcy, the Crokes' keeper, never took

his eyes off the ball, but unfortunately, neither did big Johnner Purcell, the Crokes' full back. The two Crokes' players clumsily collided.

The ball clattered off Big Johnner's left shoulder and into the path of the Barnfield full forward.

The number fourteen snatched the lose ball in his hands and thumped it into the back of the Crokes' net.

GOAL!

Mick glanced across the field. He could see Tommy Dempsey almost break-dancing with joy.

Jimmy patted Mick on the back.

'No worries, boss!' encouraged Jimmy. 'Our boys will bounce back.'

Unfortunately, Jimmy was wrong. The Barnfield centre half forward caught the kick out and sent the ball back toward the Crokes' goal, scoring a brilliant point.

Things went from bad to worse. The Crokes' defence lacked discipline and that allowed Barnfield to add two more points, bringing their score to 1-3, and still the Crokes had hardly got the ball out of their own half.

Both Danny and Jonathon worked hopelessly to get the ball up to their forwards, but Barnfield was simply on their game and it seemed as if the Crokes could do nothing about it.

Occasionally, Danny would look over toward his line to see if Trinity was cheering him on, but not once did they make eye contact. In fact, it looked to Danny that Trinity wasn't even interested in the match. At one point, she and Lowry even took Heffo for a walk.

Danny heard his name being called. It was coming from Jonathon, who had robbed the ball from the Barnfield right halfback.

Danny sprinted into a space, but he knew Deco Savage was trailing him.

Jonathon kicked a low pass along the ground, right into the path of Danny's run.

Danny pulled off a spectacular pick up and was just about to send a high one into his full forward line when Savage knocked the ball from Danny's hands.

The ball fell away from both Danny and Savage.

The Barnfield centre half back had left Doyler and come out to collect it, but Danny wasn't going to give up that easily.

Seeing Danny sprinting towards the ball, the Barnfield number six lashed out his boot to kick the ball away. Danny bravely dived with both hands stretched and marvellously blocked down the kick, ricocheting the ball out to Jason Delaney, the Crokes' right full forward who had moved in towards the action.

CRASH! The Barnfield centre half back's leg followed through and caught Danny full force in the face.

Danny rolled over twice, then lay still – no movement, no sound.

Mick and Jimmy raced onto the pitch.

Trinity and Lowry had just come around the bend of hedging at the top end of the pitch when they noticed all the commotion.

'God!' said Lowry. 'I hope that's not Jonathon. Mammy will have a fit!'

Trinity laughed, but when they got closer, they noticed that Larry had his hands on his head and Regina had an arm around Granny Maureen.

'I think it's Danny,' said Lowry, seeing Jonathon standing behind Jimmy.

Trinity and Lowry joined Larry and Regina. Trinity looked terrified. *Please let him be all right!* was written all over her face.

And Danny was all right. In fact, after a few seconds, he was sitting up and Mick was splashing water into his face.

'Ouch!' Danny complained.

'You're going to have a shiner there, Danny,' Jimmy joked.

Mick put four fingers out in front of Danny's face.

'How many fingers am I holding out, son?' asked Mick.

'Eight,' Danny joked. 'I'm alright, Da. Let me up.'

Danny was a bit wobbly on his feet.

'I think we'll take him off, Jimmy.'

'No!' protested Danny with passion in his voice.

Mick looked at Jimmy.

'We'll keep an eye on him,' Jimmy said.

'Very funny.' Danny let out a laugh.

The small gathering of players dispersed as Mick and Jimmy returned to the line. Danny's eye was swollen but he was fine and more determined than ever to turn this game around.

There was no free kick awarded as it wasn't seen as a foul, so the referee threw the ball in between Jonathon and Sean Dempsey. Jonathon won the ball and immediately fisted across to Danny who was being marshalled by Deco Savage.

Danny swiftly turned Savage and sent a perfect pass into Barry Sweeney who out-jumped his marker then did a Barry Sweeney special and kicked the ball high over his head for a super point.

Finally, the Crokes had scored, but it didn't stop there.

Doyler caught the Barnfield kick out. He couldn't find any space to shoot, as the Barnfield centre half back was glued to him, so he kicked the ball out to Splinter who flicked it up and swerved a beautiful shot over the bar.

The referee had one last look at his watch, then blew his whistle.

The Crokes players jogged over to the line. They were behind by a score of 1-3 to 0-2.

Jimmy rallied around all the players, while Mick sat Danny down near the training bag to have another look at his eye.

Heffo kept jumping up on Danny's lap and licking his face.

'Get off Heffo, ya mad thing ya,' Danny said with a laugh.

Trinity popped her head around a couple of players beside Danny.

'Would you like me to take him?' she asked, smiling. 'Oooh! That looks nasty.'

Danny lowered his head.

'Lift your head, son,' Mick complained; he was trying to hold an ice pack up to Danny's face.

Trinity slipped away.

'That wasn't very nice,' Mick said.

'I don't know why she bothered to come to the game.'

Mick wasn't going to take that conversation any further. He had a team to organise and a second half to get on with.

* * *

Danny had a little look around for Trinity as the referee blew his whistle for the second half. He felt bad for being rude to her; then he put her out of his mind. He would talk to her at the end of the game and try and sort things out.

Danny jumped for the second half throw in and beat Deco Savage to it. He fisted it over to Jonathon who immediately kicked a long pass up field before Dempsey could challenge him.

There was a battle in the Barnfield defence for the first few minutes of the second half which resulted in the Barnfield left half back fouling Jason Delaney, the Crokes number thirteen.

Danny stepped up to take the free kick and he sent it straight over the bar for a point.

That brought the score to 1-3 to 0-3 in favour of Barnfield.

The match had turned into a great contest of determination and bravery on the part of both teams. Neither wanted to admit defeat and the rivalry between the clubs was greater than ever. Barnfield had beaten the Crokes early in the season on their own pitch, but the Crokes had beaten them in the semi finals of the Féile during the summer. This was almost the seasonal decider. Victors today would be second best in the under-fourteen's division 1, but that was becoming part of local GAA history and would be reported in the sports column in the following day's local gazette as

'The Battle of Littlestown!'

* * *

There were only five minutes on the clock and Barnfield and the Crokes had both added two more points each.

The score was 1-5 to 0-5 in favour of Barnfield. Everything was going to plan for the away team.

But Danny wasn't going to give in too easily and he was making his own plans to change that score.

Danny had dropped back into his own half to pick up a long pass from Karl O'Toole, the Crokes' left half back.

Danny beckoned Jonathon in towards him and little did Jonathon realise as he ran closer to his cousin that he would be involved in one of the best GAA moves his team had ever pulled off.

Danny fisted the ball over Sean Dempsey's head and into the hands of Jonathon.

Jonathon looked up and kicked out to Brian

O'Reilly, the Crokes' left half forward. Brian dropped the ball, but with the Barnfield right half back chomping on his heels, the Crokes' number twelve regained his composure and made a perfect pick up.

He turned and looked out to his right and spotted Jonathon, who had moved into a free space.

The Crokes' left half forward hand passed the ball to Jonathon, who then hand passed to Danny who was running along side him.

The ball had made its way back to Danny and he was going to do something wonderful with it.

Danny powered forward. Clara's nickname was in the front of his mind – *Tiger Boots*. Danny felt like a tiger and the pitch was his territory. He was about to move in for the kill!

His solo brought him right into the heart of the Barnfield defence. The Barnfield centre half back thought Danny was going to shoot for a point so he jumped in the air with both hands above his head.

BIG MISTAKE!

Danny tricked him and stepped to his right, then fisted a pass out to Jason Delaney, his right full forward.

Delaney returned the pass to Danny, slipping the ball past the Barnfield full back.

Danny Wilde caught the ball and BANG! GOAL!

Danny had started that epic move and finished it with one of the best goals that the Little Croker had ever seen.

The Crokes' sideline erupted. They were level. All they needed was a draw to clinch the runner up spot. Their keeper kicked the ball out for the last time in the game as the referee blew his whistle.

The game was over.

* * *

Sean 'Dirty' Dempsey and Deco Savage could

only hold their heads in their hands in total humility as Danny's teammates picked him up and carried him over to all the Crokes' supporters.

Tommy Dempsey reluctantly followed the celebration and when he caught up with Danny, the Barnfield man reached out his hand. In it was the twenty euro he had promised Danny if the Crokes managed to finish ahead of Barnfield.

Mick stood proud beside his son. He was expecting something nasty from Tommy.

'That was one of the best scores I've ever seen,' said Tommy. He then he turned and walked away.

Mick threw his arms around Danny. 'You're dynamite. Do ya know that?'

Danny smiled. He knew he had done something spectacular, but he'd also done what Mick had said in the dressing room before the match:

Enjoy your football and you'll always be a winner!

* * *

Eventually, the crowds dispersed, the nets came down, and all the players carried their celebrations off the pitch and into the dressing room.

Danny noticed Trinity heading back to the car with Lowry. He didn't want her to leave without making things right so he raced down the grassy banks after her.

'Trinity!' Danny called.

The girls stopped and turned around.

'Can we talk?' Danny asked Trinity.

'Sure.'

'Is everything all right with us?' asked Danny.

'You seem off with me. I don't know what I did wrong.'

'We're fine.'

'Look, did I do something wrong? I don't understand!'

Lowry butted in.

'What about *Clara*?'

Danny switched his eyes from Trinity to Lowry.

'Clara? What's she got to do with this?'

'Is she your other girlfriend?' Trinity asked.

'What? I don't believe this! *No, she's not!*'

'Then why are you e-mailing her? "Tiger Boots"!' Lowry hissed.

Trinity went bright red. She could see the confusion on Danny's face.

'I'm sorry. The other night, your computer was on.'

Everything became clear to Danny. He'd left Trinity with his computer before their trip to the cinema, and she'd looked at his email from Clara.

'You read my e-mail. That was private. That was none of your business.'

'I only read the first couple of lines. The screen switched off then. I know it was none of my business. I'm sorry, Danny.' Trinity wished she had never begun to read Danny's e-mail from Clara and she wished she had never said anything to Lowry.

Danny was furious.

'Clara's just a friend. She's my dad's friend's daughter in Boston, and she's not well. That's why we – the whole team and my school – have been having collections and football marathons.'

Trinity looked at Lowry as if to say that now was probably a good time to leave them alone; Lowry bowed out.

'I'm sorry, Danny,' said Trinity, looking mortified.

Danny walked over to her. He knew how Trinity must be feeling at this moment. Trinity hung her head in shame, but Danny put his hand on her arm. She looked up at him and he smiled at her.

'Wait here,' he said, and ran off for the dressing room.

Chapter Twenty

Good News for the Wilde Boys

Danny brought Trinity back to his house.

'Have a seat,' he said as he switched his computer on. 'I should have told you all along about Clara.'

'It's okay, Danny,' Trinity said. 'This is all my stupid fault. I should have trusted you and it was wrong of me to look at your e-mail.'

Danny started typing really fast.

'What are you doing?'

'I'm writing an e-mail to Clara, but I want you to read it before I send it.'

Danny wrote:

How ya, Clara!

It's Danny. I hope you're well! Sorry it's taken me a week to get back to you, but you said in your last e-mail that you were going into hospital for some treatment so I wanted to wait until you were feeling better. I hope you're okay now. It's great news that you were given a date for your operation. I just know it will be a success and then you can get back to playing GAA and all the other stuff you love.

We had our football marathon in school last Tuesday. It was brill! But my class didn't win. Dirty Dempsey's class won. That's no problem, though, because we drew with Barnfield in the last game of the league today and that was enough to make us runners up. You should have seen it. It was savage! I scored a goal at the end to level the game. Tommy Dempsey even came over after the match and gave me the twenty euro toward your collection, and more or less said well done!

Anyway, Clara, I have someone special sitting beside me. It's my girlfriend, Trinity. She's the best! I think that you would get on great with her. She's kind, funny, dead smart and she means a lot to me. I hope you get to meet her some day.

So I'll see you next weekend. I'm really excited. I've never been on a plane before, but I'm sure it will be animal! Did I tell you that I dreamt a few weeks ago that I was travelling on a big plane with my da, and now it's going to happen? Strangely, I also dreamt that I had brought something with me - something that never leaves my room – my signed Dubs' jersey. I'm going to bring it and give it to you. I know it will mean a lot to you, being a Dubs' fan.

That's it for now. My da's just come in. See ya next week.

Danny
Tiger Boots!

Trinity read the e-mail then turned to Danny and smiled, her eyes watery. As they looked at each other, Mick came into the sitting room all excited and out of breath.

'Danny,' Mick gasped.

'What's up?'

Mick had a smile on his face – a proper smile. One that Danny hadn't seen in a while.

'You're not going to believe it, son. Hi, Trinity.'

'Hi, Mr Wilde.'

'What?' Danny asked, anxiously.

'That Principal of yours, Mr Dunnigan–'

'Dunstan.'

'Yeah! Dunstan. That's the name. He was at the game. You're not going to believe what he's after just saying to me.'

'What?' Danny let out a laugh.

Mick clapped his hands and danced around in a circle.

'He's after telling me that the school caretaker is retiring, and he offered the job to me.'

'SAVAGE!' Danny cheered and danced in celebration with his father as Trinity laughed with joy.

Finally, the future was beginning to look good again for the Wilde boys of Littlestown.

Have you read the first two books about GAA player Danny Wilde?

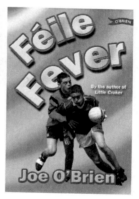

Turn the page to read an extract from *Little Croker*, the first book about Danny Wilde and his team, the Littlestown Crokes ...

The Match Against St Agnes' Boys

Mick Wilde's boys, in all-blue, lined up against the boys in red and green from St Agnes' Boys. Each player, from Paddy Timmons at right corner full back to Danny in midfield, right up to Doyler in full forward, anxiously awaited the throw-in.

Mick tied Heffo's lead to his bag and began his routine pacing up and down the line, while Jimmy just stood with his arms folded looking relaxed.

'Here we go,' announced Jimmy.

'Come on the Crokes!' shouted Mick.

'Ready, lads?' asked the ref.

Then he gave Danny and the St Agnes'

midfielder a nod. Danny and his opposite number raised their heads as the referee blew on his whistle and threw the ball high above them.

Danny was first in the air stretching his left hand above his opponent's. He passed the ball down to Sean Dempsey, then turned his man and headed for goal, leaving the St Agnes' number nine dazed with Danny's pace. The battle had commenced!

Dempsey kicked straight up to Barry Sweeney in centre half forward, who knocked a perfect pass out to Splinter Murphy.

Splinter threw a shimmy around his man and spotted Danny running in behind the full forward line.

Danny raised his hand.

Doyler made a run wide and opened up a gap for Danny.

Splinter knocked a sweet pass in towards Danny, who caught it beautifully on the run.

Danny took a quick glance at goal and

dropped the ball onto the side of his right boot.

The ball swerved past their keeper and into the top right corner.

GOAL!

'Come on, lads!' shouted Danny as he fisted the air in glorious celebration.

Mick and Jimmy were hopping around on the side line.

'What a dream start!' cheered Jimmy.

'Come on lads, settle down and back into it!' warned Mick.

Jimmy was right – Danny had given the Crokes the perfect dream start and it totally rattled the St Agnes' boys.

Barry Sweeney caught the kick out and knocked a long, high ball over for a point.

Crokes kept the ball in St Agnes' end of the field for the next twenty minutes, scoring four more points. Danny was playing a stormer in midfield, winning everything in the air and when they tried to break through, Danny relentlessly pulled off tackle after tackle.